# MAGGIE...
## WOMAN OF ROBERTS COUNTY

A NOVEL

Char Jarman

MAGGIE...Woman of Roberts County
Copyright © 1999 by
CHAR JARMAN

ALL RIGHTS RESERVED

Library of Congress
Catalog Card No.:99-93020

ISBN: 1-57579-148-x

Printed in the United States of America

PINE HILL PRESS, INC.
Freeman, S. Dak. 57029

## DEDICATION

Dedicated to A. J.,
without whose help and encouragement
this would never have been finished.

## ACKNOWLEDGEMENTS

Historical information from the writings of H. S. Morris, Samuel J. Brown, and the Minnesota Historical Society.

Picture of the courthouse in Wilmot taken from *Wagon Wheels,* Volume 3, by Norma Johnson.

Newspaper quotes from *The Dakota Sun,* Travare, D. T. October 30, 1884. South Dakota Archives. (The name Markham is fictitious.)

Picture of T. H. Peever from the book, *Sisseton, South Dakota,* from the Sisseton Public Library.

# Travare

As you drive the winding road that leads into Browns Valley from the south, (we call it The Short Cut), you will pass a deserted farm on the left as you round the first curve. All that remains are clumps of ragged trees, a sagging clothesline, and a small silo with a caved in barn beside it. These mark the homestead of one of the first leading citizens of Roberts County. A bit further you will see a well kept farmstead of older buildings on the right, then the road will take you down the hill into Minnesota.

Next time you drive this way, look closer. Let your imagination see a thriving young town, with this road as its main street. Look across the field to the east and see a stately building with a limestone foundation. See a hotel...stores...offices...a school...homes, for once this was the first seat of the newly organized County of Roberts, Dakota Territory. It was the center of the hopes and dreams of a small group of pioneers who dared to plan...maybe even scheme, to fulfill that dream. Although the dream didn't last, it still lives on in the minds of those of us who love history.

Mention is made of some actual historical figures including only: Joseph R. Brown, Samuel J. Brown, Mrs. Samuel J. Brown (Phoebe), Chief Gabriel Renville, and T.H. Peever. All other characters and personal names are fictitious

The names of towns and townships, however, are real.

# CHAPTER 1

**Chicago...1883**

"Giddap there!" the driver called, and flicked his reins impatiently as the horses plodded wearily through the muddy streets, drawing the carriage to the train station. Clouds hung ominously over the tall gray buildings as if promising more rain yet that day. The people hurrying along with their heads down looked as gray as the weather and the buildings. Huddling under my warm coat, I pulled the veil more securely around my face to keep out the cutting wind and moved to the middle of the seat to prevent the mud from hitting me. Some of it was finding its way through the open windows and I breathed a prayer of thanks that we didn't have much farther to go. Just two more blocks and I would be on my way to freedom, the first real freedom of my entire life. As we neared the station, I felt a stab of guilt at having left my mother standing tearfully in the doorway, but shook it off resolutely and squared my shoulders as I stepped off the carriage. The driver signaled a porter to take my luggage as I walked into the sprawling expanse of the depot and joined the milling crowd.

There was plenty of time, so I took a stroll about the waiting rooms. I had been here many times with my parents as we took the train back to Philadelphia to visit relatives at least once a year, so it was all familiar to me. I decided to buy a packet of post cards to write on the train as there were a few of my friends who cared that I was going so far away, and of course mother. Poor mother, who never had a chance to stretch her wings, and follow her dreams. I mulled this thought around my head for awhile, then discarded it. Mother more than likely had her dream right there where I left her, her husband, house, and friends. I had been a part of it too, and it did make me sad to disappoint her and father, but it could not be helped.

When the time grew nearer for departure, I located the boarding area, and stood nervously waiting the call, clutching my ticket tightly. I had looked at it a dozen times already to check that it was right and it always was...Chicago to Minneapolis, one way. In Minneapolis I would have to buy the ticket for the rest of my journey on west. As I picked up my traveling bag and boarded the coach to find my seat, I vowed to make a new life for myself far away from this city where I was born and raised.

My mother had fretted about me taking the coach instead of a compartment, but I had to conserve money until I would be earning a paycheck. My father was so angry at my decision that he would have refused to give me anything even if I would have asked. All the money I possessed was from my former position. If it hadn't been for mother's sweet-talking, father would have disowned me completely, I believe. Not because he hated me, but that I dared to thwart his plans for me.

I settled down in my seat by the window and watched as Chicago flew past below us. The city that had been home all my twenty-five years was soon left behind, and we were gliding through Illinois farmland. By the time night had fallen and I had finished my supper of cold chicken and bread and butter that mother had packed for me, we had crossed into the Wisconsin woods. I leaned back in my seat and tried to sleep, but the past kept coming back until I finally gave in and let the memories take over.

My discontent with the life I had been brought up to really took root and began to fester the night of my coming out ball. Four other girls from our circle of acquaintances were being presented to society at the same time. This was the night the young women were shown like prize cows at a state fair auction. The buyers being the eligible bachelors who stood self consciously along the sidelines, taking careful note of their good and bad points.

I had no illusions about my looks and stared at my reflection in the train window remembering that night...standing in front of the long mirror in my bedroom gazing despondently at my tall bony frame swathed in yards of white organdy that made me look ridiculous. I had pleaded with mother to let me choose a simpler dress that would suit me better, but she wouldn't hear of it. She insisted all the girls were wearing white ruffled gowns, and I would stand out unfavorably in anything else. My thick brown hair was the one good feature and it was done up rather well I had to admit, but...my pointed nose and firm chin...Well, they were a legacy from Aunt Matilda. These combined with deep-set brown eyes did not make a face that would launch a ship, or even a rowboat for that matter. All the other girls were dimpled little creatures that could flirt prettily with the young men and talk nonsense while batting their china blue eyes. I never had gotten the hang of batting my eyes, and if I could think of anything to say it was usually about something I had read in the newspaper or a bill passed by Congress. Yes, I was quite hopeless as a debutante. "Margaret," my poor mother would sigh in exasperation, "You must learn to curb your interest in these things. You know politics is the man's domain, and he does not want to hear opinions on it from a young lady."

I got through the evening without disgracing the family and myself, and the bachelors danced dutifully with all of us. However, I squirmed with embarrassment inside my white organdy thinking this was the night some of us would be singled out for courtship. As it happened, I needn't have worried, because after one or two duty calls, the young men lost interest in me. They would sit and twirl their waxed mustaches nervously while perched uncomfortably on mother's horsehair sofa in the parlor. The talk was mostly trivial nonsense, and if I tried to discuss anything interesting, such as the news of the day or what was happening at City Hall, they would look aghast. Then more than likely my habit of laughing at the wrong time would overtake me, as I saw their embarrassed expressions. I was a grave disappointment to mother and father who had visions of me making a good match with one of the sons of their well-to-do friends.

Once my parents realized the suitors were not beating a path to our door, they agreed that I could take a position teaching some of the young children of the families in our neighborhood who did not attend the public school. I was happy with this and enjoyed being responsible for the children's lessons and deportment. In my spare time I read the newspapers and tried to keep up with what was going on in Illinois and the country. I also continued to study history and arithmetic, as well as grammar and penmanship. My dream was someday to be a real teacher and have a class of my own, or work in the office of someone in a government position. Oh, I had high hopes for the daughter of a Chicago businessman who had made a fortune in grain speculation on the side. Mother was the president of her garden club and much involved with church and charity work. These interests befitted a matron of society, and their only daughter was expected to follow in her footsteps and marry well. This meant into a family of good name and fortune.

When my father finally faced the fact that I had no interest in these pursuits, he began mapping my life out in another way. I was going to be sent to Philadelphia to spend a year with relatives, the plan being that I would meet a man who was willing to overlook my shortcomings and marry me. This was not said in so many words, but it wasn't too hard to figure out the intention. Anyway we were soon at odds, with mother caught in the middle. Every day I searched hopefully through the paper for job opportunities for young ladies in my position, but there were none in this year of 1883.

I did not give up, however, until one day something caught my eye. "Needed...Teacher, in a newly organized town in Dakota Territory. Many other job opportunities will be available also. Apply by letter and send credentials." Well! Now there was something with possibilities. Thankful for the teacher's certificate that I had, I went to the library, took down the big book of maps and looked up Dakota Territory. It seemed to be very far away and the wide expanse of land was quite townless. Well, this is an older map, there are no doubt many more towns than are listed I assured myself. The idea had caught my imagination and I could not forget it. At last I got up courage to ask my employers for letters of recommendation and wrote to the name listed in the ad...C.B. Preston, Travare, Dakota Territory.

## CHAPTER 2

As the train sped on through the darkness, the motion at last began to make me sleepy, and the next thing I knew daylight was breaking through my window. Looking around self consciously, I saw the other passengers beginning to stir, and knew I must look a fright after a night spent sleeping in my traveling suit. I gathered up my bag and unsteadily made my way down the aisle to the washroom at the far end of the car. There I took my hair down and redid it the best I could in the cramped quarters. I peered into the small mirror noting the line of worry between my eyes and tried to wash it away with cold water. At last there was a rapping at the door and I had to make room for someone else. Shrugging ruefully at my reflection, I opened the door and made my way back to my seat. Finally the call came that breakfast was being served in the dining car, and I gladly went in search of a hot cup of coffee and something to eat. My cold supper of last night seemed a long time ago.

After breakfast, my old spirit returned and I began to enjoy the ride through the rolling hills and small towns of Wisconsin. Looking around at the other passengers, I realized more than ever that I was the only woman traveling alone. But I had expected this, and just let the adventure ahead occupy my mind instead of the fears I probably should have had. When the view began to tire me, I took a book out of my bag and began to read about the land where I was going.

Even the name promised adventure...Dakota Territory...The town of Travare. What a romantic sounding name. Was it French? It had said in the advertisement that it had recently been named the seat of the county government. That alone seemed to assure a prosperous future for the new community. People would come to town for their legal business and stay to buy from the local merchants. I was looking forward to seeing this up and coming little city on the prairie.

Putting my book down, I thought back to the day the reply to my letter had arrived. It was dropped on the hall table with the other mail when the maid had answered the postman's ring. Other mornings I had made it a point to be at the door when he arrived so as to intercept any letter before mother and father got to it. Today I was late coming down, but I knew if a reply were coming it would have to be soon. I looked over the stair railing in time to see mother shuffling through the letters and stopping at one and staring at it with interest. "Oh no," I groaned inwardly, and tried to saunter casually down the stairs. "What's in the mail today?" I asked, in a hopefully uncaring tone. "This came for you dear," replied mother with a questioning look. As I took it, one glance at the postmark told me it was what I had been waiting for. I went back upstairs to my room and closed the door, as with shaking hands I tore open the envelope. "Dear Miss Sinclair," it began. "This is in reply to your application for the teaching position. Thank you for your interest. When I placed the advertisement, I had in mind a man would only be acceptable. This is a rather unsettled territory yet and not really a place for a young lady accustomed to city life. But in the absence of any other applicants I am offering you the position, at least on a trial basis. If you find it too difficult, it will not be held against you if deciding not to stay. If you do wish to accept, please send a wire as soon as possible. The train connections are good this time of year. From Minneapolis, you will come west to Browns Valley, which is the end of the line. This is only one mile from Travare, and there is free transportation from the station to our town. We have a good reasonably priced hotel where you may stay temporarily, but once the school term begins, it is customary for the teacher to board with the members of the school district. I will be awaiting your reply. Very truly yours, C.B. Preston."

    With mounting excitement, I read the letter three times before I could believe it. My passport to a new life! My ticket to freedom! I felt like jumping up and down and yelling out the window, but suddenly it occurred to me what this meant. I had secretly answered the ad and now it was up to me to go down and tell my parents what I planned to do. At this thought, my hands began shaking again and I felt like a guilty child having to confess a wrong-doing to the two people who meant the most in the whole world to me.

    Muttering a brief prayer for guidance under my breath, I slowly crept down the stairs with the letter in my hand. Father was going to the office later this morning, so they both would be reading mail in the library. I would have much preferred to tackle mother first, like the coward I was at the moment, but there was nothing to do but face them both. They looked up at me as I opened the door and went to stand by the fire, hoping the warmth would make me quit shaking. It didn't, so finally I just walked over, handed the letter to father and waited for the explosion. He must have read it three times as well before the message began to sink in. He looked first at me and then at mother, as he demanded, "Did you know about this Abigail?" She took it from him and scanned it quickly before confronting me in distress. "Margaret, what on earth does this mean?" "I am leaving," I said flatly. "I had made up my mind that if I was offered the job I would take it. I'm sorry, but I won't be sent to Philadelphia, and there is nothing here for me." "What do you mean, nothing here for you!" father thundered angrily. "You have not given one of these young men a chance. You scare them off with your modern ideas and talk of politics and other things that are strictly a man's province. I really don't know what to make of you Margaret, where you get your ideas is beyond me!" He threw my letter down in disgust. I took a deep breath and tried to tell him how I felt. "Father, there isn't one man in our whole group of friends who interests me. With their silly talk and soft hands and spoiled ways, I can't stand the sight of any of them. When I marry, I want a real man, one who isn't afraid of my ideas and of me. If not, I shall remain single. I'm sorry, but that's how I feel, and I am sending Mr. Preston my reply today. I would like to go with your blessing," and I looked at them both sadly, "But I am twenty-five years old, and if I don't find my own life soon, it will be too late. I'll end up just being an old maid governess to other people's children the rest of my life. Oh, I do want to get away, and see new country and different people, can't you understand that?" I picked my letter off the floor and went into the hall and closed the door. I leaned against the wall with heart pounding, trying to calm myself, then went to the closet for my coat and hat. I had to take the carriage to the telegraph office, where I sent my reply, then to the station to inquire about schedules and buy a ticket.

    With that done there was nothing more but go back home and think what came next. I needed warmer clothing, that was certain, and a few more practical dresses. I had an idea my morning and afternoon frocks would not be entirely suitable. I did have one or two gray teacher's dresses that I wore when working. Two or three more plain dresses of that sort would do, along with some warm underwear and stockings. I had boots for walking in the snow as Chicago was nearly the same kind of weather as Dakota Territory. It wasn't as if I was going to a foreign country after all. I had plenty of dressy gowns of the latest fashion for eveningwear, but doubted I would need all of them. Money was definitely going to be a problem, as I had a good idea that father was not going to finance this expedition. Nearly all my wages were in an account since living at home I scarcely had to spend any. This was another guilty thought, that I had lived off my parents for much too long. I should have done something on my own years ago instead of drifting along.

When I got to the house again, I went to find mother and tried to reassure her that I was making the right decision. She wasn't angry, just sad, that I felt I had to leave. I asked if she would come with me to do the errands at the bank and my shopping, but she was afraid that father would be angry if she appeared to be helping in any way, so I went alone.

I found the clothing that would be needed and a few items that might be hard to find in a small town. My luggage was new, from the trips we had taken recently, so that was one thing I didn't need to buy. I packed all the cases with as many of my possessions as they would hold, the days before leaving. There was a heavy box of books that I used for teaching and some that I had studied from when a child. Remembering something my mother had done when we went on a trip east, I sewed a cloth pouch that would fit around my waist under my petticoats to hide most of the money. Then I would only have to carry as much as was needed for the journey in my handbag. I didn't relish the prospect of being robbed by some unscrupulous person enroute.

At last there was nothing to do but wait for the day of departure. My father was like a stone wall and would not budge on his opinion of my going. He scarcely looked at me or spoke during this time. I could almost feel sorry for him...being so set in his ways that he would let his only child leave with no word of advice or to tell me he loved me in spite of it all. I knew that I was a big disappointment to both of them, but all I could do was hope that in time they would forgive me for wanting something different in life.

I looked up from my thoughts when the train whistle blew and the conductor came through the car calling that the next stop was Minneapolis. It didn't take long before we were at the station and I had to make certain all my luggage would be changed to the next train. The porter pointed out the direction to the ticket office, and as I asked for a one way ticket to Browns Valley, the agent looked at me oddly, "Miss, are you sure that's where you want to go? That country is hardly civilized yet!" I tried to look as dignified as possible and assured him in what I hoped was a haughty tone that I most certainly did know what I was doing. So he shrugged his shoulders as if washing his hands of the matter and handed over the ticket.

As I boarded the coach for the last leg of my journey, it was rather disquieting to see the other passengers who would be joining me. Mostly unkempt and disreputable looking men, the likes of whom I had never seen before. Some were carrying long rifles, which the conductor insisted be put in the baggage car. There were spittoons on the floor of the aisle, and many of the men were using them with varying degrees of accuracy. I turned my head away in disgust and stared fixedly out the window rather than encounter the curious stares of the other passengers.

After some miles, I began to notice a change in the landscape, and forgot everything else while watching the rolling tree covered hills change to rolling, treeless prairie. So this is what Dakota Territory looked like. I was fascinated with the scenery, but with fall beginning, could well imagine what it must be like here once the winter snow and winds came.

I must have slept for some time because when I awoke the sun was beginning to slip below a ridge of hills that were visible in the west. The lamps were lit in the coach and as I looked around some of the men were dozing, some playing cards, and others just waiting for the journey to end. The conductor came through to tell us we were nearing Browns Valley, and I began stuffing my books and things back in my traveling case. By this time I was ravenously hungry again, and surely hoped there would be supper at the hotel.

As the train pulled to a stop at a wooden building beside the tracks, I had my first look at the town of Browns Valley. What I could see didn't amount to much but in the dark it was hard to tell what was beyond the depot. In reading about the area I learned that it had been a trading post as early as 1866, so for this part of the country was already well established.

I was relieved to see the horse drawn bus waiting beside the station, and the conductor and driver loaded my heavier bags and boxes while I took some of the lighter ones. I climbed aboard feeling more grubby and disheveled than I could ever remember. There were only two other passengers going on the carriage, both with tobacco stains running down their chins and their possessions in burlap bags. We pulled away shortly, and followed the road over a bridge that crossed a narrow river, then out of town. It was completely dark by now but the moon gave enough light to show that we were climbing a hill to the south, and at last I could see faint lights ahead. We drove up to the door of what the driver told us was the hotel and stopped. It was only a two-story frame house from what I could see, but I was thankful to get out on solid ground again.

"Here you be, missy," grinned the driver as he unloaded the last of my belongings onto the porch of the hotel. "They'll hep you get it inside later," and he touched his cap as he disappeared into the night. The two tobacco stained ones had melted into the darkness of the street beyond the hotel.

Taking a deep breath, I opened the door that led into a dark hallway. Peering into the gloom, I noticed a crack of light under a door to the left, and cautiously rapped. I could hear plates clattering on the other side and immediately the door was flung open by a young boy. He gave me one look and yelled over his shoulder, "She's here, Ma!" and to me, "Come on in!" A young woman with a harassed look on her face hurried over wiping her hands on her apron as she ushered me into the kitchen. "Oh! I'm sorry I dint have the lamp lit in the hall fer ya, it gets dark so early now, I plumb fergot. You are the new teacher aren't ya?" She peered into my face questioningly. "Yes," I answered tiredly, "I'm the new teacher, at least I hope so." "Well, I ain't heerd they hired anyone else, so you must be," and she gave me a friendly smile. "We been waitin' for a school to open fer a long time here, and we'll be right grateful if ya take the job. It won't be no bed of roses, I expect," she added. "But here now, I'm keepin' ya from your supper, and you probly dying for somethin' to eat." As she chattered, she was setting a place for me at the kitchen table and stirring something in a pan on the stove. She pointed out the wash basin on the other side of the room, "You go ahead and wash while I heat this up again. The others et in the dining room earlier, so hope ya don't mind sittin' here in the kitchen. Warmer here anyways." "I don't mind a bit," I told her at once. "And you are right, I am starving...I didn't have anything since morning." The good smell of food warming almost made me weak in the knees as I went to wash my face and hands.

While I ate the young woman kept up her lively talk, but at last she stopped and clapped her hand to her forehead. "Lan sakes! Where's my manners, I haven't even told you my name...I'm Sofie Johnson, and this here's my boy, Ben," and she held out her hand. "Charlie told us your name, Miss Sinclair. Me and my man, we run this hotel and Ben helps out what he can cuz Luke has a couple other jobs besides, but it's a purty good business." She finally paused long enough to catch her breath. "You can sure tell I ain't had eny woman to visit with for awhile, mostly menfolks stop here so far. But tell me 'bout you and what it's like where you come from." I knew I would like this talkative woman, and hoped that she would be a friend to me in the days ahead.

At last I began to yawn, and Sofie noticed immediately. She hustled me to a room upstairs, while she and Ben hauled my luggage off the porch. The room was plainly furnished with bed, dresser, wash stand, and one straight chair, but the sheets were white and fresh smelling, and I knew I would sleep like a baby here tonight.

# CHAPTER 3

When at last I awoke the next morning, the sun was beginning to peek through the windows. I jumped out of bed and went to look out at the town. A few false fronted buildings made up what looked to be the main street over to the west, as I tried to peer around as far as I could. On a hill facing the northwest was a two or three story building with large windows that I assumed was the courthouse. That was about all I could see except for the line of blue to the west that was the beginning of one of the lakes I had read about. Sofie had knocked on my door while I was looking out. She was carrying a bucket of hot water, so I happily bathed and dressed. I hung two of my new dresses on the hooks by the door, wore one, and left the others in my suitcase, as I wasn't sure how long I would be here. One last glance in the mirror, and I was ready to face my first day in Travare, Dakota Territory.

The wonderful aroma of hot coffee wafted up the stairs as I made my way to the kitchen, where I found Sofie busy frying pancakes and salt pork on her huge range. She glanced up as I came through the door, and smiled in her friendly way, "There you are, Miss, you can sit in the dinin' room this morning, the others are already at the table, here, I'll pour ya a cup o'coffee first." And she took a huge gray enamel pot from the back burner and poured the lovely steaming brew into a thick mug. "Why don't you let me help you take these in?" I offered, after my first gulp. "Oh, Miss," she protested, "You oughten to do that, you're one o' the guests." "Nonsense," I said firmly, "I'll be glad to give you a hand, and don't call me Miss, I'm just plain Margaret. When I'm a teacher, I'll be Miss Sinclair, but not to you, I hope. Now if you'll point me to the dining room, I'll take these to the men." I picked up the platters of hot cakes and fried meat and went to the door. Sofie grinned at me gratefully, and motioned to the second door down the hall. "You're right, I'll be glad o' the help this once, I'm runnin' a little behind," and she hurried back to put more cakes on the griddle.

I opened the swinging door with my hip and strode over to deposit the platters on the table. The talk and laughter died suddenly as eight pairs of male eyes turned to see who had come in. They all gawked at me in silence until I offered a curt "Good morning" and left in a hurry.

"Sofie, is it all right with you if I eat out here in the kitchen?" I asked hopefully. "Aw shucks, Margret, those fellers won't bite, they just ain't used to a city girl like yourself bringing in their pancakes!" and she chuckled in amusement. I looked down at the dress I was wearing, one of those I had chosen carefully so as not to look too out of place, and she laughed again. "Well, you do look purty spiffy this morning, but if you want to eat out here that's fine with me. I'd like the compny. Those guys in there would probly be tongue-tied anyway, if you went to sit with them." She set a plate in front of me and heated up my coffee from her pot.

The kitchen door swung open then, and a husky, dark haired young man came in carrying two pails brimming with milk. "Here you are mother," he said as he set them down, "The old girls outdid themselves this morning!" As he turned to me, Sofie introduced us, "Here's the new teacher Luke, Margret Sinclair. This is my husban'" she added, to me. "You dint get to see him last night, he was workin' late shovlin' grain at the elevator in Browns Valley." Luke Johnson looked me over unsmilingly and shook his head, "I told Charlie he was out of his mind hiring a city bred eastern girl to teach the school, and now I'm sure of it. You're much too young and good looking for the job," he finished curtly, and poured himself a cup of coffee. "Luke! Shame on ya, embarrassin' Margret like that, what's got in to ya this mornin?" Sofie scolded. "That's all right, Sofie," I replied, "I realize I'm a city girl, but not an easterner!" I protested heatedly, "I'm from Chicago...that's not the east. I'm not all that young either! I told Mr. Preston in my letter I am twenty-five. Besides, I hope I have the sense to learn the ways out here and make a good job of teaching. Anyway, no one ever told me I was too good looking before so I don't believe it for a minute!" And I buried my red face in my coffee mug, as Luke burst out laughing. "Oh my! Old Charlie is going to get a surprise when he lays eyes on you, I can hardly wait to see his face." "Why, what do you mean?" I demanded. Luke didn't say anything until he got a plate out of the cupboard and speared on three pancakes. Sitting at the table and pouring on the syrup, he answered, "Well, you see, out here a woman of twenty-five is usually well past her prime...and looks it, excepting my Sofie of course," he added hurriedly, as he eyed his wife holding the rolling pin threateningly. He swallowed another mouthful and continued, "The land out here is hard on women, and a lot of them don't last. Charlie has been here most of his life, and he's seen how it goes. Lots of the women either die young or go back east to their families. Sofie and me, we have this place, so she doesn't have to work in the field like a lot of them. It's hard work here too, that's for sure, but at least we can hire help with the heaviest jobs." I sat in my chair digesting this information and wondered silently about "Old Charlie." Would he send me packing when he saw me? He better not even think of it, I told myself...I would not go back to Chicago without having at least the trial period he had promised me.

"When will I be meeting Mr. Preston, do you think?" I asked, trying to hide my nervousness. "He said yesterday that he would stop over here this morning before he goes to the courthouse," Luke answered. "Why, what does he have to do with the courthouse?" I wanted to know. "Didn't he tell you? He's head of the county commissioners. He has an office over there, but he isn't in it only for meetings. He delivers the mail, writes the newspaper, and runs the mercantile down the street besides." "H'mm" I thought sarcastically to myself, a man of many talents." Aloud I observed, "Do all the men around here have several jobs?" Luke just laughed good naturedly, and replied, "We're pretty unorganized here yet, and there are lots of things that need to be done. Besides everyone, or just about everyone, is trying to get enough money together to get hold of some land of their own. We're expecting that in a few years the Indians will be moved off this reservation here and it'll be opened up for homesteaders." "Well!" I retorted. "That sounds rather harsh! Where will the Indians go then?" Luke just shrugged and went on with his breakfast, "I dunno, move further west I suppose. They agreed to it and they'll get paid for the land so what's the difference where they live?" "No doubt it will make a great deal of difference, in the long run," I said, more to myself than to him. "Now until our Mr. Preston gets here, I will help you with these dishes Sofie," and excused myself to go upstairs to find an apron.

Sofie and I were nearly done washing up when through the kitchen window we saw a man stepping on to the porch and wiping his feet outside the door. "Here he is!" she hissed at me, and raising her voice, called out, "We're in the kitchen Charlie." I took off my apron and folded it slowly as I watched the door open and the tallest man I had ever seen ducked his head automatically as he walked in. "Charlie," Sofie said by way of introduction, "This here is the Miss Sinclair you been expectin'." He strode over to offer his hand, looking down at me thoughtfully, "I'm happy to meet you miss," he said politely, "I trust your journey was not too tiring?" I looked at him in surprise as his speech sounded more like a Philadelphia lawyer than a backcountry storekeeper. "Very well. Thank you," I answered, while looking up at him in amazement. To tell the truth, I had been expecting a middle-aged man sort of like my father. This man was nothing like my father, not in the slightest.

"May we talk here at your table Sofie?" this giant asked politely, "And might I have a cup of your most excellent coffee Ma'am?" "Oh go on with ya, Charlie Preston, I'll get ya some coffee, but you be nice to Margret here, she and I are friends already, and we're gonna stick t'gether. High time s'more women got to this town to soften things up a bit." After saying this piece, she slammed a cup down on the table in front of him, filled it, and whisked out and up the stairs.

"Well, well," C.B. Preston said under his breath, "Looks like you have a staunch supporter in our Sofie." "I think she is a fine lady," I said primly, "I shall be proud to call her my friend." "Have you had a chance to look around town yet?" he asked, taking a pouch of tobacco out of his pocket and beginning to roll a cigarette. "Oh, sorry miss, do you mind?" "No I don't mind," I told him. At least it isn't the kind they chew, I thought with relief. "Actually, all I have seen is from the windows this morning," was my reply. "It was dark by the time I arrived last night. I did see part of a street, and the building over east must be the courthouse?" "Yes," he answered proudly, "We built the foundation from limestone made ourselves in the kiln on the hillside. This is going to be a fine little city eventually, and I'm glad to have had a part in it."

"But we have to talk about the school and if you think you will be really up to teaching in this wild country. Of course it's tamed down a lot since I first came in '64, then it was mostly fur traders and Indians." "You must have been very young then." I thought I had said it to myself, but somehow it came out my mouth. "Sixteen, and ready to conquer the west," he chuckled. "My folks had died back east and I just wanted to see some new country. I liked it here by the lakes. I took up a trap line, learned to speak Dakotah and did pretty well. Lots of beaver and other fur bearers back then." He spoke softly, while looking into the past, like a much older man would. Then he seemed to remember who he was talking to and came back to the present. "As I was saying, are you absolutely sure you want to do this? I know I said you should try it and no hard feelings if you changed your mind, but it would be very disappointing for the parents if you started and then didn't stay. I would rather buy your return ticket today and head you back to Chicago on the next train east." "I listened to this speech until he was finished and then replied calmly, "All right, Mr. Preston, you have had your say, now I will have mine. I answered your ad in good faith. I was fed up with society life in Chicago. I taught children and was good at it, but wanted a new life. A life where I would be a real person instead of just Alfred Sinclair's daughter. Old maid daughter, I might add. I intend to teach your school and hope I can do it successfully, if not it won't be for lack of trying." And with that I looked him straight in the eye with the look that used to send the young men running for the door. C.B. Preston didn't run for the door. However, he snorted with laughter, and nearly choked on his cigarette smoke as he raised his arms in surrender. "All right, Miss Sinclair, you've convinced me. Come for a ride and I'll show you the new school building. Where's your coat and hat?" I was so surprised by this turn of events that for a couple of seconds I had no idea where my coat and hat were. At last I gathered enough wits to say I would only be a minute and hurried upstairs to get my wraps. Sofie was making a bed in one of the rooms, and I stopped to tell her quickly where I was going. She gave me a wink and told me to watch out for that Charlie, he was a devil with the ladies. "Thanks a lot Sofie, I'll keep that in mind," I muttered hurrying down the stairs.

The morning was fine as Charlie helped me into his buggy that was tied to the porch railing. He lifted the reins and spoke softly to the bay mare waiting patiently for him. "What a beautiful horse!" I couldn't help exclaiming. "Where did you get her?" "I bought her as a colt from an Indian that lived above Lake Traverse a few years ago. She and I have gone many miles together already. She's a good faithful friend, Little Bird. She had a Dakotah name, ke-TAH-lah ze-T'KAH-nah, and that's how it translated."

As we turned the corner by the hotel I had my first full view of the town, and blinked in surprise. There was not much to see. I counted seven or eight business places at the most lined on either side of a narrow street. A few houses and stables and of course the court house. Besides the hotel that was all there was to the town.

We followed the trail to the southeast, past a few more houses and one or two sod shanties. Playing out in front of one of the homes were two children who waved happily as we passed. "They will be a couple of your students. There should be around ten in all if they come." Out about a quarter of a mile I caught a glimpse of a tiny unpainted frame building standing by itself except for two small out houses. I glanced questioningly at him and he nodded, "That's the school, we got it built this past summer in the hopes we would get someone to teach. These children are going to need some learning if they are ever going to amount to anything. Some of the folks teach them at home, but others haven't got much schooling themselves, some can't even read. I suppose you wondered why we had to advertise for a teacher, but there just aren't that many qualified around these parts yet. Browns Valley has their school, with four teachers, but we needed our own building and school board in this county." He turned into the schoolyard and pulled in front of the door. "I have the key with me, so I'll show you what it's like inside." He unlocked the door and held it open for me. Directly inside the door was a narrow entry way the width of the building. On the wall were pegs for coats, and at one end a wash stand and a place for a water bucket. "Of course the water will have to be brought inside once winter is here. There are more coat hooks inside too, to keep the children's wraps from being frozen when they put them on. Some will have a long walk morning and night."

The schoolroom itself was well lit with windows along both sides. Three rows of desks faced the front of the room where the teacher's desk and chair stood. Behind that was a blackboard made of slate, with chalk and an eraser already placed on the ridge below. A few books lined the shelves on the other wall. There were even framed pictures of the Presidents, Washington and Lincoln, on either side of the black board, and an American flag stood in the corner at the front of the room. A round clock was on the wall beside the bookcase, and I turned to Charlie and remarked,"Well, it certainly looks as if you have thought of everything!" He grinned like a small boy and replied, "I wasn't sure what you were expecting, but we tried to put in most of the things you would be needing. I know we are short of books, but some of the families have books at home to bring, and I believe you mentioned you have a number of your own." "Yes, I brought all those I used in my teaching and some I had when still in the classroom, so we should have enough to begin." I answered. I walked over and took down two or three of the books; there were readers, some arithmetics and a couple of geography books with colored maps.

"I suppose this is a lot different than the school you are used to in the city," Charlie observed watching me. "Not many girls go to public school in the area we lived, mostly we were tutored privately. That is how I got my teaching certificate, and was able to go on and tutor other children in their homes. I actually haven't had any experience in a public school, but I expect it won't be all that different." Charlie's eyes opened wide at my naïve statement, but all he said was, "I'm sure you will manage just fine, and if anyone gives you too much trouble, just let the school board know, and they'll sort it out, they won't put up with troublemakers." "I would hope nothing would be that serious surely!" I protested, "These are just young children after all, aren't they?" At this Charlie looked a little uncomfortable and didn't quite meet my eye as he mumbled something about two or three of the boys being a bit older. "How much older are we talking about here?" I demanded, catching his sleeve and forcing him to look me in the face. "Sixteen or seventeen, maybe, but," he added quickly, "they won't be going the whole term anyway, just when the work is done on the farms and they don't have trap lines to see to or something." All of a sudden I felt as if I had made a ghastly mistake and sat down on the edge of the teacher's desk and closed my eyes wearily. "Sixteen or seventeen year old boys...well..." I eyed Charlie cautiously. "What else should I know that you haven't told me?" He cleared his throat a couple of times before he went on. "It's expected that you will either walk or provide your own way of getting to school and back each day. We still plan to put up a stable for a horse or two as some families have an extra horse their children can use. And there is the matter of getting the fire lit and kept going. The parents will provide the fuel, but it will be up to you to have the fire burning before the pupils get here. Do you think you can manage that?" For the first time I noticed the pot bellied stove standing at the back of the room. All of a sudden there flashed before my eyes the lovely feeling of coming downstairs on a winter morning to a roaring coal fire that had been built by the hired help long before we were awake. "All right, you wanted freedom," I told myself sternly, "So forget about that." "Of course, I can manage!" and flashed a big smile that showed my teeth, but I doubt it erased the worry from my eyes. "Well then, I'm sure you will do just fine. As soon as we have a little more money allotted, we will provide more material. You really should have a few reference books."

As we drove back to town, he took me on the street past the courthouse, which was a beautiful new building. "One day you can come on over and look around, but for now I have to get you back. I need to go to the Valley to pick up the mail before our meeting at the courthouse." "Does the mail go out every day?" I asked, as I needed to write mother and father to let them know I had arrived safely. "The train runs every other day on this line and brings the mail from the east. From the west it has to be brought by team and wagon from Wilmot." As he dropped me at the hotel door, he waved to Ben who was bringing in wood, and as he drove away called out, "I'll be stopping by later, Miss Sinclair, see you then." I stood watching him drive away, feeling a bit sick in the pit of my stomach. I had to talk to Sofie right away!

## CHAPTER 4

I walked into the kitchen mulling over everything Charlie had said. Sofie was busy preparing the noon meal, so I tied on my apron, and offered to help peel potatoes. "What did ya think o' the new school? The fellas did a great job of it din't they?" "Yes, they did," I agreed, and at last getting my courage up, blurted out, "Sofie, how do you light a fire?" She looked at me blankly for a moment before bursting out laughing. "Oh you pore little thing! I wondered when I saw ya with your nice clothes and purty hands how much of this stuff ya knew how to do. But never you mind, I'll show ya how to get a fire lit tomorrow mornin' if ya get up early. Its no big mystry, just need dry kindlin', a bit of paper, and if the draft is right, you'll have a roarin' ol ' blaze in no time. Jest don't open the drafts too much and let it go up the chimney, or ya might set the roof afire." I looked at Sofie fearfully, but she just grinned and gave my arm a squeeze, "Come on, don't look so scairt, you'll learn in a jiffy. Anyways nobody has burnt nothin' down since we been here." "Well then," I replied hastily, "I certainly do not want to be the first! I wouldn't care to be around Charlie if I burned his precious schoolhouse. He would pack me off on the first train east for sure!" Then I thought of something else, "I am going to have to buy a horse to ride, I don't have a lot of money, but will have to see what I can find." I was talking more to myself than to Sofie, but she answered me anyway, "There's a couple horse traders in the Valley, Luke could go with you one day if you needed help pickin' one." "There's another thing too that I wondered about. Charlie mentioned it in his letter, but I forgot to ask him today. He said teachers board with people in the district, what does that mean exactly?" I asked, setting the kettle of peeled potatoes on to cook. "I guess where schools have been started round here, families take turns boardin' the teachers for free. Some folks hereabouts aren't so well fixed and don't have even a speck o' extra room, so the ones who have will do it. We was thinkin' since we have plenty room most of the time, we would take an extra turn. You could kinda make this your home away from home too on weekends, no charge o' course." She added hastily. "If you'd be willin' to help out some, I'd sure 'ppreciate the compny." I looked at this generous little woman while a lump gathered in my throat, "Look here

Sofie, I have enough money to get by, and after the first month will be getting a paycheck. I will be glad to make this place my home on weekends and vacations, but not without pay. It just wouldn't be right. I'll be happy to help you as much as I can anyway." Sofie just smiled at me and replied, "We'll just let it go fer now and not worry our heads 'bout it all right? Now I got to get this meat fryin. We got three men that come back here to eat on noon, and the four of us, not so many as at night."

So I set the table and then went upstairs to unpack some things. I took out the books and set them on the dresser, thinking I should be making lesson plans. Without knowing the pupils and what grades they would be in, there was not much I could do about that however. I sat down to think quietly, and that's when I made the decision not to buy a horse. I certainly could get up early enough to walk to school and I had good warm clothing for when it really turned cold so I wouldn't freeze. With that off my mind I breathed a sigh of relief, and went on with my unpacking.

After dishes were done, Sofie and I went outdoors and she showed me the barn where Luke had milked the cows that morning. Ben was busy cleaning out as the cows were turned into a small fenced in corral where there was still some green grass. Luke had haystacks piled beside the fence for when winter came, Sofie told me. Next we stopped at the chicken house where the eggs for the kitchen came from. I had never picked a freshly laid egg in my life, but there in the nest were warm brown eggs to put in Sofie's basket. There were a few small trees not far from the hotel that were beginning to turn golden, and some leaves had already fallen. The sky was a brilliant blue with just a white fluffy cloud here and there. Looking into the distance I could see Lake Traverse to the north and Big Stone Lake to the east. This is beautiful country, I thought to myself. No one should go hungry here, with the fish in the lakes, the wild game to hunt, and land to raise grain, corn and vegetables. But of course, I knew of the droughts and grasshopper hordes that plague the prairies. There are things in nature that can wipe out an entire summer's work, and not a thing can be done about it.

The next morning I was out of bed and down to the kitchen at the same time Sofie came yawning in to get breakfast started. She jumped a little when she saw me, and shook her head as if to clear it, "Lan sakes, I plumb forgot ya were gonna learn 'bout lightin' a fire today." But she bustled over and clanged the lids on her kitchen range, at the same time checking the supply in her wood box. "Alright now, your stove at the school looks diffrent, but it'll light the same way." She handed me some newspaper and told me to crumple it a little and put it in the firebox. Then she said, "Take some of those fine wood chips and put over the paper." She gave me the box of matches, and told me to light the paper. It flared up at once and I jumped back in alarm. "That's fine," my teacher assured me, "We'll jest set this lid back on part way till the kindlin' gets goin'." After a minute we peeked in and the chips were beginning to burn. "Now you put a few pieces of the bigger wood in, but not too much at once, or it'll smother and go out." Having done this, I watched as Sofie got the coffeepot filled with water from the bucket that Ben had brought in the last thing after supper. She took off the back stove lid once the fire was blazing and set the pot directly over the heat. Then she busied herself with other breakfast preparations. "How many this morning?" I asked. "Seven, besides us family," she replied. "See? I'm already callin' you family!" "You are a dear, Sofie," I told her honestly, "I'm so glad you are here, you have been such a help to me."

By this time the fire was hot enough so she told me to add more wood and close the drafts some. "You come down again tomorrow, and see if ya can do it by yourself. Luke does the big stove in the dinin' room when the weather gets colder, but we don't need it yet. That one burns hard coal. You will mor'n likely have coal at the school. Ya start it the same way, but after the wood is burnin' hot, then add the coal. Coal is nice, 'cause it lasts longer than wood."

"Here, you wanna mix the pancakes this mornin'?" Sofie offered, setting out eggs and buttermilk and a huge bowl. "Uh, oh, of course," I mumbled quickly, "Your recipe is here some place?" She just laughed and pointed to her head, "In here, but never mind, I'll tell ya what goes in when. First break in a dozen eggs and beat them good with a fork." Having done that, "Pour in this pitcher of buttermilk, a few cups of flour to start, couple tablespoons soda and baking powder, and beat up good with the big spoon. Oh ya, don't forgit a couple teaspoons salt." Muttering the ingredients to myself, I somehow got them into the bowl and beat them together. "That looks purty good, maybe jest a titch more flour," Sofie observed as she tossed in another handful. "Oops, sorry!" she exclaimed as some of it flew into my face. "Quite all right," I chuckled, wiping it with my apron, "Now, what's next?" "The griddle is heatin' and as soon as the sausage is done, we can start fryin'. The men'll be comin' in purty quick. The water is 'bout ready to put the coffee in." I watched as she measured two cups of coffee into a small bowl, cracked in an egg, added water and mixed it all up with a fork. Then she carefully stirred it into the pot of boiling water and watched as it began to bubble up. After stirring it again, she put the lid back on and moved it to a cooler spot on the range. "There, that'll be ready in a few minutes. Never wanna boil the pot once the coffee is added, jest let it sorta steep, brings out the flavor but don't turn bitter." So that's how she makes that delicious brew, I thought to myself, another lesson learned. For a teacher, I was doing more learning than teaching so far.

This morning when Luke brought in the milk I turned to say good morning, and he laughed out loud at my flour-speckled face, but I didn't care, I was enjoying myself more than I had for years.

The days until school started passed quickly with helping at the hotel, studying the lesson books, and going for walks on the hills. Sunday, only a meal for the family was prepared as the four of us piled into Luke's wagon and drove into Browns Valley to church. Since the night of my arrival, I had been to town twice, and had decided that my first opinion of it being not much of a town was quite true. There were a number of buildings scattered about randomly; some were businesses, one a post office, and the depot of course. There was an artesian well that was the town's water supply. The church we went to was the Episcopal that Sofie said had been started soon after the town began. Nearly everyone went there, some Indians too, who had been converted to Christianity.

Browns Valley, besides being situated by what was called the Little Minnesota River, was between the two lakes. Charlie told me that some years when there were heavy rains or a lot of snow melt in the spring the town would flood. He also told me about this area between the lakes being the continental divide, with Big Stone Lake running south into the Mississippi, and Traverse eventually emptying into the Red River which ran north to the Hudson Bay. "Didn't you know that, teacher?" he teased. "No I did not," I was forced to admit. Imagine that, a river that flows north, rather unusual in continental United States.

Monday morning Sofie told me, "No helpin' this morning, you can tonight, if ya feel up to it, but you have your job to do now, so jest hurry up and eat. I made some sandwiches for your lunch and here's an apple to put in too." "Thanks Sofie, I'll make my own sandwiches tomorrow, you have enough to do in the morning." So with my books and lunch bucket, I set out. It promised to be fine weather, and Sofie thought to tell me before I left that I wouldn't be needing a fire the whole day, just to take the chill off this morning. Unless the wind changed to the north.

As I was striding along enjoying the crisp fall air, a buggy pulled up beside me and Charlie leaned out smiling, "Like a ride first day of school Miss Sinclair?" "Why thank you sir," I answered in my most schoolteacherish voice and grinned back at him as he gave me a hand up. "Wish me luck today," I said, "A few prayers wouldn't hurt either!" "Oh don't worry, you'll get the hang of things here, you've all ready been teaching, so all you have to do is fit it in to a different kind of people than you are used to." "I guess so," I answered uncertainly, "I hope the pupils like me." "Why ever wouldn't they?" he wanted to know. "I'm not thinking of the little ones, I'm sure I'll be fine with them, it's the big boys I'm worried about. I'm not used to big boys, what if I can't handle them if they decide to make trouble?" "Just remember what I told you," he answered as he pulled in front of the door, "The school board will stand behind you, and I'm sure the parents of the boys will, too. I don't think any of the big ones will be starting yet, there is still work getting ready for winter on the farms and they are needed at home." "Well, thank you for the ride and the encouraging words," I told him as I climbed out and took the key from my pocket. As I opened the door and turned around to wave, he called "Goodbye! See you soon!" What a nice man, I thought, wishing I'd had a brother like him. He's so different than the men I knew in Chicago. Imagine, coming out here at sixteen, and living on his own. None of the simpering idiots I knew could have done that.

Giving myself a mental shake, I prepared to face my day at school, no more day dreaming, lots of work to do. First get the fire started.

That evening, while helping Sofie get supper ready, I told her about my day. After all the worrying, it had gone quite well. The fire started without trouble and ten pupils were there by nine-o clock...ages six to twelve. The entire morning was taken up with learning about each one and where to place them in grades. One of the eleven year olds knew almost nothing about letters, but was very good with numbers, and the six year old could read from the third grade lesson book. So it would be interesting and I was looking forward to the next day. Young Ben Johnson would be started at third grade as his father had been teaching him reading and writing, and he was anxious to learn more. Ben had waited for me after school and helped sweep up the room, then walked home with me. "Just this once," I cautioned him, "Because your mother needs you for evening chores."

# CHAPTER 5

The sunny fall days went by quickly, and one early November morning we awoke to snow falling heavily and a chilly southeast wind. I had to face into it walking and was glad of my warm coat and scarf. This morning there were four older boys who came, so now I had fourteen pupils. I had a large knot of uneasiness somewhere in my middle, as I looked the new- comers over. Two of them were tall as grown men, and I was sure I saw tobacco chews wedged in their cheeks. They were from three different families, so one of the tallest boys and the smaller blonde one were brothers. Their names were Jim and Jonas Berger. The other two were Levi Parker and Arnold Mac Pherson. Their folks were all farmers in the district.

I had tests prepared for when they would come, so had them work on them in the morning. While they were out for noon hour, I quickly looked them over. Jonas appeared to be at about seventh grade level and the others fifth and sixth. It was obvious they had not had much schooling at home or anywhere else. The problem was that they would be in classes with younger students, and this might not set too well. But there was no getting around it.

So I went to work with my new pupils, and right away Jim balked at being put in the same recitation class with an eleven year old, but I stood my ground, and told him as soon as he passed that reader he could move up, so he had to be satisfied with that. We had six grades now that all had different lessons, and it made a full day. We had classes in reading, spelling, arithmetic, history and geography. Twice a week the older ones studied government from a book that I had learned from, and on Fridays we practiced drawing and penmanship.

The pupils were mostly well behaved and polite, but one day Levi and Arnold began teasing two of the younger ones who were sitting in the desks ahead of them. I nipped it in the bud at once, but then Levi spit on the floor in the aisle as if to show me I could not get the best of him. At this my blood began to boil. Keeping my temper the best I could, I ordered him to clean it up with a rag that was used to wash the blackboard. Standing over him with the look that father once said would peel paint at twenty paces, he finally gave in and with one swipe, cleaned up the disgusting mess. With pounding heart I went back to the second grade spelling class. What would I do if he really defied me? I wondered, but for now he had his nose back in his book and appeared to be reading.

No more incidents happened that day and I breathed a sigh of relief when the last pupil was out the door. As I went about the chores of sweeping the floor, and cleaning erasers, I made up my mind that these boys were not going to disrupt the school. The other children were settling down to the routine of classes and I was beginning to see progress with them.

Ben must have spilled the beans to Sofie about what had happened that day, because she looked me over carefully as I came into the kitchen and dumped my books tiredly on a chair. "You alright tonight Margret?" she asked in concern. "Yes, Sofie," I sighed, "Just a little weary in the head." "Here now," she said briskly, "I had some cocoa made up for Ben when he came home, and I kept some hot. That'll put th'starch back in ya!" So I sipped the rich chocolate drink and felt the strength slowly oozing back into my tired brain and body. "Thanks Sofie," I breathed gratefully, "This really hit the spot. I'll be down in a minute to help with supper as soon as I get my apron," and headed for the stairs.

It seemed that every day I helped in the kitchen it was to learn something new. I hadn't realized before how ignorant I was about the everyday work of running a home. I had been taught to give orders to the cook and other household help, but had never needed to do as much as make my own bed before now.

And as each day went by, teaching got a little easier. The pupils and I got to know each other, and eventually, they were confident what was expected of them. The big boys even behaved fairly well, after a brief mutiny following my ban of chewing tobacco during school hours. The day after this law was put into effect, I had a terrible time getting the stove lit. It had been working so well; that I couldn't imagine what I was doing wrong. The smoke all seemed to be coming back into the room instead of going up the chimney. After checking the drafts for the third time, I finally had to go outside and leave the door open to air out. By this time the children were coming, and Bobby Anderson asked, "What's the matter teacher? The stove is smokin' something awful!" "Yes I know," I answered, "I just can't seem to get it to burn this morning." One of the older boys noticed right away that there wasn't any smoke coming out where it was supposed to. "Acts like the chimney's plugged," he said. "I'll climb up and have a look." The roof wasn't very high, so we rolled a barrel over that stood beside the door.

He climbed like a monkey and grabbed hold of the chimney and pulled himself up. "Lookit this!" he exclaimed "Somebody put a board right over the opening, no wonder it didn't draw!" He took it off, dropped it to the ground, and immediately smoke began pouring out. As he climbed down he remarked, "I know who did it too, and bet they don't show up at school today." He was right; none of the four big boys came. I had a little talk with the others and suggested nothing be said about it at home. We would just let them stew in their own juice for awhile. They would be waiting for a wrathful teacher to come tattling to their parents, but since it had turned out all right, I would say nothing either. They could just wonder what happened. After three days of silence, apparently they couldn't stand it anymore and came back to school. No one let on a thing, but I made sure they had all their missed lessons to work on during both morning and afternoon recesses.

## CHAPTER 6

Holiday time was approaching and Sofie was busier than ever in the kitchen doing special baking. It would be the first Christmas I had not been with my family, but I still did not feel ready to talk to father. Besides the trains were unreliable during the winter when the snow got deep and I wouldn't risk not getting back after vacation. Mother wrote once a week and I did too, so that she would know that things were going all right for me. Luke even found a scrubby evergreen tree somewhere and brought it in for us to decorate, so the downstairs of the hotel began to look quite festive.

Two weeks before Christmas, Sofie told me about the community dance in the hall in the Valley. Everyone was going, she said, even the children. "Oh my, I don't think I will be going," I protested, "I never had much fun at dances." "But you have to! Everbody will expect to see ya there. You can't jest sit home alone!" That evening Charlie stopped by to talk business with Luke and as he was leaving he stopped to speak to me for a few minutes. Just as he was going out the door he turned around to say, "Will you allow me to escort you to the dance Saturday night?" I was so surprised I stood like a fool gaping at him. "Why would you want to take me to the dance?" I demanded. "And why not?" he laughed, "You're the prettiest woman around, and besides you can be fun when you leave off those prissy school marm ways." "What!" I sputtered, "I'm never prissy acting!...am I?" I finished uncertainly. "No, not really, I just said that to get your dander up so you'd forget yourself and say you would go with me. Come on, say you will, it'll be fun. There'll be fiddles and guitars, a good old hoe down." I couldn't help laughing at the boyish expression on his face and finally said I would be happy to go with him.

Saturday morning, Sofie, Ben, and I carried water and refilled the reservoir on the kitchen range, besides filling the big wash boilers and setting them to heat on top of the stove. This was routine every Saturday at Sofie and Luke's where the water had to be all hauled in from the well out by the gate. Sometimes they could use soft water from the cistern, but this winter the cistern had gone dry already. We made a supper that could be put in the oven so as not to need all the burners for cooking. Once supper was over and dishes done, we all took water to our rooms and had baths and got dressed for the big night. I brought out one of the party dresses I had packed, not knowing if there would ever be a use for it. I had to admit it felt good to get dressed up again after so long.

Promptly at eight Charlie called for me in his sleigh. Luke, Sofie, and Ben would be coming behind us in their bobsled. There were jingley bells on the horses, and it was a lovely ride down the snow-covered hill into town. The hall was at the west end of town, and there was already a row of sleighs, bobsleds, and wagons around the building. There was a barn at the back to stable the horses, so they didn't have to stand in the cold.

The band was tuning up as we walked in. It was only a group of the local fellows who knew how to play. There were two fiddles, a guitar, and an accordion. I had to admit it didn't sound too bad. I hadn't known what to expect, as the only dances I had ever been to were formal balls, with string orchestras. At the first waltz, Charlie came to collect me and we joined the others on the floor. He was a very good dancer, and I caught a few envious glances from some of the younger girls who were being herded clumsily around the floor by their partners. After that we danced a couple of polkas, and then sat down to have some cider while we caught our breath.

While we were sitting the next two dances out, Charlie told me about some of the people from the area that I had not met. Then he mentioned the Browns, who lived nearby in the big log cabin by the river..."Sam was our postmaster for quite a few years," he explained, "And now he runs his own business here in the Valley. I'll tell you an amazing story about him when I get back." And he went to refill our cups at the other end of the hall.

When he returned and sat down he told me the tale of the young man, quarter breed Indian, who was head of the scouts at Fort Wadsworth in the 60's. A report had come in by runner, of hostiles in an area north of there. He rode as fast as he could to the Elm River scout headquarters, which was fifty-five miles west of the fort. When he got there he found out it was a false alarm, and fearing there would be bloodshed because of the wrong information, he saddled a fresh pony and started back. Before he was anywhere near Fort Wadsworth, a blizzard came up and he got way off course to the southeast. At last he was able to recognize landmarks and realized where he was. By the time he rode into the fort he was in bad shape. He was between life and death for a time, but finally pulled through. He never did walk again without help though. He was crippled from that time on. "But,"

Charlie went on; "He didn't let it get him down. He moved here and has had a good life. Found a wife in St. Paul and brought her here to the Valley." "Was the town named for him, then?" I asked. "Actually, it was named for Sam's father, Major Joseph R. Brown who had a trading post on Lake Traverse in the early days." Charlie answered. "He had been chief of scouts before Sam, which was only one of the many things he did in his lifetime. But that's a whole other story. For one thing, the log house was used as scout headquarters at the fort. When they were finished with it Joseph R. moved it down here piece by piece and put it back together. It's made of solid oak, so should last for years."

"There must be a lot of colorful history in this part of the country," I remarked, "I want to learn all about it eventually. Luke tells me the reservation might be opened for settlers, that the Indians agreed to sell it to the government." Charlie frowned thoughtfully, "I know, that is the plan all right, there will be people from everywhere trying to grab a claim, then some of the Indians will move further west I suppose. They do get to keep a certain number of acres each for themselves." "You don't sound as if you approve," I observed, looking at him sideways. "Oh I don't know what's the right or wrong of it, but it just seems to me the Sioux are giving up the best of the hunting and fishing land. Lake Traverse and the hills west of here with all the lakes. If they get moved further west than Aberdeen, like to the other side of the Missouri, that's some mighty sorry land out there. Come on, let's not worry about things we can't do anything about, we came to dance, didn't we?" and he pulled me back to the floor.

We all rode back to Travare singing Christmas carols in the frosty night air. It had been such a happy evening, meeting new people and especially spending time with the ones who had become like family to me. Ben was nearly asleep as we all pulled up to the hotel and Luke helped him get inside while I told Charlie goodnight and thanked him for asking me. "The pleasure was all mine, Miss," he intoned politely, and then gave me a wink. "We'll do that again sometime soon, I hope," and was off into the night with a jingle of sleigh bells.

## Chapter 7

There were two full weeks of vacation after Christmas, and once the second half of the term began, I left my comfortable room at the hotel and went to stay with a family out in the township. They were the Hansens, Lars and Inga, and were farmers with a few acres. They also had some milk cows and chickens. Three of their children were my pupils, so we would walk to school together each morning. They didn't mind that it would be cold when they got there, and I was glad of the company on the mile walk. The boys had to get up early enough to help their father with the chores, and the little girl was busy with sweeping and doing the breakfast dishes until time to leave. Their house was a claim shanty originally, with two rooms added, so they had a little extra space.

Lars and Inga had brought their family from Sweden just five years ago, they told me. They were looking for land of their own and a freedom they did not have in the old country. As we would sit in the kitchen and drink coffee around their table, they told of the hardships that the early settlers faced at that time. They had come by covered wagon from the east with all their worldly possessions. Olga was just a baby of two, and the boys had to help with caring for the horses and making camp every night on the trail. They came with six other families, and someone always kept watch at night for raids from bands of hostile Indians. I grew to have a great admiration for these sturdy people who carved out a life for themselves in a strange country, with its extremes in weather. Hot, dry and windy in summer and cold, snowy, and windy in winter.

Inga kept a tidy house in spite of bare floors and cramped space. My bed was in a tiny room that I shared with Olga, and being on the north side of the house, the walls would coat with frost. But we had soft handmade quilts and a feather bed for a mattress, so we kept warm. Inga would wrap bricks that had been heated in the oven and put them at the foot of the bed. That would warm the sheets enough to make it tolerable when we gingerly stuck in our toes. Once again I thought of the lovely room and cozy bed of my old life. I had no regrets though, and relished each new experience as I learned more and more about Dakota Territory.

The neighborliness of the township and the residents of Travare never ceased to surprise me, being used to city life where one did not associate with anyone but one's own class of acquaintances. The businessmen seemed no different from the farmers and the commissioners were ordinary people who farmed or had other jobs or businesses. When there was a house party it was an open invitation for any who could come.

One Saturday night, early in March, Inga and Lars planned a party with dancing and card playing. There would be a fiddle and accordion for music. The furniture was shoved together as much as the limited space would allow, making a tiny dance floor. Inga had baked cakes and some of the other women would bring things to eat for later in the evening too. Usually I walked back to the hotel for weekends, but this Friday night I stayed to help Inga get ready for the party. All day Saturday we swept and dusted, and piled everything that could be gotten along without in the bedrooms. Inga had bread rising early in the day and when it was ready she showed me how to shape it into loaves. A kettle of eggs was put on to cook for egg salad sandwiches, to go with the cakes and a pot of coffee would be made for the hungry group later.

The chores were done early that evening and after a cold supper, everyone got ready for the big night. The house was full by 7:30 and still people were arriving. I wondered where in that little shanty everyone was going to find a space to stand, let alone dance. But by the time the music started, there was a spot cleared in the middle as if by magic. People sat or stood in the kitchen. One group was playing cards at the table, and the children were everywhere. Some learning how to dance, others sitting along the wall watching, and still others were playing a game quietly while three babies slept beside them on the bed. Coats were piled in the corner of Olga's room, and once when I went in to find a hanky; there were four girls from school sitting on the bed talking. I was greeted happily and even teased a little, as one of the older ones asked slyly if teacher's beau was here yet. I just laughed at them and said that teacher didn't have a beau, and went back out to dance. People had begun to think of Charlie and me as a couple, and sometimes it crossed my mind that he would make an ideal husband for the right girl. But I was not sure if that right girl was me...yet. Maybe I am destined to be an old maid, I thought dismally to myself as I looked around the room at all the smiling couples with their children. But I knew from the short time I had known these people that all was not sunshine here either with life and marriage. Over in the kitchen was one husband who drank too much, playing cards with another who at times spent the butter and egg money gambling at the pool hall in Browns Valley. Sitting alone along the wall was a wife who had almost lost touch with reality. Folks shook their heads when she was mentioned and wondered what would become of her family. The hard life had taken its toll on some of those who just were not strong enough. Her man was thinking of packing up and taking them back east, Sofie had told me. "Maybe for the best," was her thought, "Before she goes completely crazy and hasta be taken away." I shuddered at the mention of the insane asylum, as from childhood we had heard the grown ups whispering about the disgraceful conditions of these places.

    I shook off the bad feeling these thoughts brought up and went to help Inga get the lunch ready. She had made the big pot of coffee and there was cold fresh milk for the young ones. I marveled at the way these country women took entertaining in stride and didn't get upset if they only had plain food to serve. It reminded me of mother planning a dinner or afternoon tea, where everything had to be lavish and the table decorations perfect. If the least thing went wrong it ruined everything for her. Here no one minded if a glass of milk spilled, or a cake didn't turn out just right. The milk was quickly wiped up without fuss and the cake covered with sugar frosting and no one knew the difference. There were too many life and death matters to worry about insignificant details.

    The children fell asleep after eating their snacks and the party went on until the wee hours of the morning. My feet were sore from dancing, but it was one of the best times I ever had. I never dreamed parties could be so much fun.

    Sunday morning was spent helping Inga put the house back to rights and then we all went to church in their bobsled. The sun was shining brightly on the snow as we glided down the hill into Browns Valley, and Inga, Olga and I sang some of the old hymns as we rode along.

    In the afternoon everyone had a nap to catch up from our late Saturday night, then Inga and I made a light supper for the family while Lars and the boys milked the cows. At the table the family was already planning what they would be planting as soon as the ground was ready. It had been an unusually mild winter, and now in March the snow was nearly gone and green grass beginning to show underneath.

## CHAPTER 8

March 20th began as another sunny warm morning and I noticed two flocks of geese heading for the north as I walked to school. I was now boarding with another family in the district who lived nearer the school. These were the Carlsson's, another Scandinavian family, who only had one child enrolled.

After the pupils and I had eaten our lunch we all went outdoors to enjoy the warm day. The children were having a lively game of kick the can as I sat on the doorstep watching them. I gazed across the hills to the lake, and it looked like the ice was going to break up soon. It had turned a dark color, and the boys had told me that when it got like that it was not safe to drive on with the horses anymore

We were all back at our desks, with the children studying quietly when the sun was suddenly gone and the wind crashed around the building. Everyone looked up fearfully from their books, and I went to the window to see what was happening. The snow was swirling by the schoolhouse in a blinding white cloud. In a minute the temperature dropped inside that thinly walled building and I hurried to put more coal on the fire. I went to the entryway to check how much fuel was piled up, and was relieved to see that there should be several hours worth of coal and quite a bit of split wood. I had been warned about these storms when the school term began, and the advice was always the same. "Never leave the building on foot during a blizzard. Too dangerous." They told me that landmarks were too far apart and it would be easy to become lost. Charlie said one day, "If you have to burn every stick of furniture in the building do it, but NEVER leave the school and expect to find your way home. You and the children would more than likely freeze to death." These words came back to me now, as I looked out the window hoping to see a let up in the storm. If anything it was getting worse, and the room was becoming very dim.

There was one kerosene lamp on the shelf and I was glad that it was full of fuel, but we would get along without it until night fell, if we were unable to leave. I asked the big boys to bring fuel inside and pile it against the wall. Then all the children brought their coats, caps and scarves inside where they could put them on if need be. They still had their heavy winter coats as their mothers made sure they were prepared. I had left my warmest shawl home that morning, because I had been so sure spring had arrived. "Fool!" I berated myself. I should have known not to trust such bright sunshine, as I had heard Sofie say more than once.

When these chores were done, I gathered everyone closer to the stove and read until the light grew so dim I could no longer see the page. Then I asked them to choose songs they liked, so we passed another hour singing. No one complained, and everyone made the best of it, even the smallest. I knew they were getting hungry, as I certainly was, so I asked if anyone had lunch left in their pails. Not everyone did, but we got out what there was and shared it. I had a whole sandwich left that I cut in small pieces, someone else had an apple, and still another a large piece of cake. Everyone got a couple of bites, and there was water in the pail, and that was our supper. After we had eaten I lit the lamp, and the children settled down next to the stove with all their wraps. Once they were asleep I would blow the lamp out to save the fuel. I could see well enough by firelight to put in more coal.

I have to say, that was the longest night of my life. My feet were like blocks of ice, from foolishly leaving off my warm stockings. The nagging worry was always at the forefront of my mind, that maybe this storm would not end by morning, but go on for days, as I had been told happens some winters. What would we do then? No food, the fuel would be running low in a few hours, how could I best protect these children that were put in my care? At last the windows began to look just a bit lighter, and I knew morning was coming. The children were fast asleep and I did not wake them. Poor things, I thought, let them sleep as long as they can. Soon enough they will wake up hungry and frightened and have to face the cold.

After stoking the fire one more time, I finally dropped off into an uneasy doze. I dreamed there was someone banging at the door and awoke with a start. The banging was a giant snow covered creature stomping its feet on the school room floor. The children began to wake and sit up. All of us stared in unbelief at the wonderful sight of Charlie Preston shaking the snow off his cap. I closed my eyes in a prayer of thanks for our deliverance and staggered to my feet. I nearly toppled over as they were so numb with cold, but managed to catch myself on one of the desks before I fell at Charlie's feet in a heap. "H-how did you g-get h-here?" I asked, my teeth chattering so badly I could scarcely speak. "The wind is letting up some," he answered. "I was at Sofie and Luke's when the storm hit, so had to spend the night. Made up my mind I was coming to get you in the morning somehow, as I knew the fuel wouldn't last much longer. I brought the bobsled from the hotel, and we will go back there and warm everyone until it gets better. I can see good enough now to find the way all right. Come on, everybody! Shake a leg! Let's get going." As the children refastened their coats and tied their scarves around their faces, I closed the drafts on the stove and prepared to leave. Of course Charlie noticed my meager wraps and had a few uncomplimentary words about it. No more than I had been telling myself. He had heavy robes of buffalo hide in the bobsled though and we crawled under them.

Charlie urged the horses into the north wind and the good sturdy animals took us over the snow banks, which by now were very hard. It didn't take long until we were at the hotel porch and Sofie was gathering her son into her arms with tears running down her face. "Aw Ma," Ben protested, "We were all right! We slept right by the stove and kept warm." "I knew Miss Sinclair would look after you all," Sofie answered, drying her eyes, "But I was jest so scairt."

As we all crowded into Sofie's warm kitchen, she passed us cups of hot cocoa. I thought nothing had ever felt so good as the warm fire and to look around and see the children all safe. I gave Charlie a shaky smile, and he nodded back, saying quietly, "You did fine Margaret, just fine." I knew then that was the finest compliment anyone had ever paid me, and had to look down to hide the tears that welled up and threatened to spill over.

When the storm was over, Luke and Charlie took all the children to their homes and drove to some of the other houses in the township to check on people. No lives were lost in that sudden blizzard, but several head of livestock had wandered off and died, piled together against a fence. When I wrote my mother that week, I was careful to make no mention of that day, as I didn't want her to fret any more than she all ready did. However I described it all in detail for my diary, so as never to forget the March blizzard of '84.

From then on the weather warmed and the snow began to melt. I walked to the edge of the hill one day in early April to see the Little Minnesota River rushing down brimming full with the melted snow from the hills. The water carried with it some logs from dead trees in the coulees that would cause a jam in Browns Valley when they got caught under the bridge. Then the men would have to use every means they had to loosen them, so the water would continue to flow and not flood the town. The ice on the lakes was breaking up and in a day or two would be gone, Sofie told me.

The school term would end the last day of April and then I would have to make the decision what to do until fall. I had been offered the job again, and I intended to take it, but the matter of my parents continued to nag at me. At last I made up my mind that I would go back to Chicago for a few weeks to visit, and perhaps then my father and I could patch things up.

The last day of school the pupils and their families gathered for a picnic on a grassy knoll overlooking Browns Valley. The water had subsided, and the green leaves were coming out. I sat munching my sandwich thinking what a beautiful place this was and how fortunate I had been to find it. The town had grown the few months I had been here. Two more businesses had started and Charlie's newspaper, *"The County Sun"* was enjoying a wider circulation as other towns in the county were selling it. Charlie sat beside me on the blanket and when he was done eating, rolled his usual cigarette, lit it and peered at me through the cloud of smoke. "Well Miss Sinclair, are you certain you will be coming back to us in a month? Or is some bright young fellow going to sweep you off your feet, and carry you back to high society? You might realize that you missed it after all." He looked at me with a question in his blue eyes and picking my hand off the blanket, examined it closely before giving it a little squeeze and laying it down again. "You and I are going to have a talk when you get back. I tried to get up my nerve before, but now I best wait till you are sure you are returning." "Oh, I'll be back, you can bet on that," I replied trying to sound casual. "You won't get rid of me so easily...In case you haven't noticed, this place has become more home to me in a few short months than Chicago did in all the years since I was eighteen." With that I changed the subject to some news of the county and we soon were in our usual discussion of the school and township happenings.

Before everyone left that afternoon, I made sure to say goodbye to all who lived out in the township as I would not be seeing them before I left in two days. My things were back at Sofie and Luke's, where I had packed just enough to see me through the month. The rest of my belongings could stay there, Sofie assured me. "You are comin' back for sure aren't ya?" She asked a little anxiously the night before my departure. "You know what, I think Charlie has gotten real sweet on ya, and hates to see ya go." "I know, I hate to leave too, but I have to see how things are with my folks, and then I'll be back before you know it." I didn't want to talk about Charlie, because I didn't really know how I felt, and needed some time away to think.

The day I left, the Travare bus took me to the station with my one suitcase. Sofie and I said our good-byes that morning, and I had not seen Charlie since the picnic, so our last words were the ones we had spoken while eating our lunch. As I looked back at the town, the strange feeling came over me, that nothing was going to be the same again. Telling myself to stop being an idiot, I faced north and did not look back again. I was only going to be gone one month, what could possibly change in that short time?

As I was standing on the platform ready to board the coach, I heard someone call my name. Looking around I saw Charlie ride up on Little Bird and hop off onto the platform beside me. Taking my hand he looked into my face with those incredible blue eyes, and said soberly, "I wasn't going to see you off, because I did not want to tell you goodbye, but something made me ride down here before the train left. Promise me you WILL come back in a month?" He looked so serious, that it made my skin cold with superstition all over again. "You know I'll be back Charlie. Unless something drastic happens, you will see me right here on this platform the last of May." He bent over and gave me a quick peck on the cheek in front of everyone, and with a wink and a wave he turned Little Bird around and was gone. With my cheeks a tell-tale shade of pink, I slunk into the car and found a seat by the window, where I could hide the tears that had begun to trickle down my cheeks.

The trip was uneventful except for having to stop for a herd of deer that had wandered out of the woods onto the tracks near Minneapolis. The train ground to a halt and we all craned our necks out the windows to see why we had stopped, but could see nothing. It was the conductor who told us what had happened as he came through the coaches before we stopped in the city.

I expected to take a cab to my parent's house from the station, but wonder of wonders! There was mother with father beside her waiting as I stepped off the train. For a woman who almost never shed tears, I was turning into a regular fountain, as I cried happily on their shoulders. Father patted me awkwardly on the back as he joked, "There, there daughter, don't get me all soaked, I wore my new suit just to come and meet you." And he chuckled in his old way. Then I knew I had my father back again. Mother was beaming all over and wiping tears at the same time, so it was a happy family that made the trip back to my old home.

# CHAPTER 9

Before I unpacked my case in the room that had been mine as long as I could remember, I went around touching the momentoes of my girlhood. Mother had left everything where they had been at the time I moved away. On the shelf stood the bride doll I had gotten for Christmas when I was eight. My ice skates hung on a hook in the closet. I must remember to take them with me when I leave. Maybe we can skate on the lakes next winter. I saw more books that the little girls in my school would enjoy reading for the fun of it when their lessons were finished. In the closet were all the beautiful dresses I had left because I knew they wouldn't be needed. Maybe I would take two different ones now, there might be some festivities at Travare this fall when harvest was over.

It was good to sit at the table with my parents again while we had dinner. But I had gotten out of the habit of sitting down and being served by a maid. Once I jumped up to get something from the kitchen and mother looked at me strangely, "Oh yes, I suppose things are done differently in Dakota Territory?" she remarked questioningly. "Indeed yes," I replied, "I have been helping Sofie make and serve the meals at the hotel when I am there." "Just don't forget that you were raised for a better life," father warned. To that I had no answer, as I did not consider the work I was doing beneath me, nor did I want to start the old argument again.

The time flew by, as mother and I called on old friends during the day, or she and I would help at charity functions. Many evenings we were invited out to dinners and parties. One night father and mother had a dance in my honor, and the house was full. As I danced with one after another of the men who had remained single in my absence, my thoughts returned to the holiday dance at Browns Valley. What fun I had there among people who knew how to have a good time after their week of hard work. It didn't take long to figure out that things had not changed here. The men were just as superficial and the girls as silly as before.

I was nearing the end of my month's visit, and getting restless and anxious to return to Travare. It had been good to see my parents and some of the old friends, but I would be glad to be back on that westbound train. I wouldn't even mind the tobacco chewers this time. I was aware mother and father had been hoping that I would change my mind and stay in Chicago, but it was never mentioned in so many words. I was sure they did not want to disturb the peaceful atmosphere between us either.

Three days before my departure, a messenger came from father's office to tell us that he had collapsed at his desk and had been taken to Saint Luke's hospital unconscious. With fearful hearts, Mother and I had the driver take us there, and the doctor was waiting as we came in. "It's his heart of course, it has been failing for some time, you knew that didn't you?" The doctor questioned us. Mother sat down suddenly with a stricken look on her face. "He never let on anything to me about it, why didn't he say something?" She began to cry softly, "He always seemed so strong and in charge of everything, I never dreamed there was anything wrong." The doctor took us to the room where he lay white and still in the bed. I bent over to check if he was breathing, and he was, but still unconscious. We stood beside his bed, mother and I, in total disbelief, at seeing a forceful man like father suddenly struck down.

We both spent several hours in and out of his room or sitting endlessly in the waiting room staring at nothing. Finally I could see that mother was exhausted, and I coaxed her to take a cab home and rest. I would stay and keep watch till morning, then if he was better, go home, change my clothes and come back.

I dozed fitfully on the uncomfortable couch, waking at intervals to walk down the hall and check with father's nurse, who was in the room all night. There was no change, until 6:00 A.M., and a flurry of activity down the hall brought me to my feet in a panic. "What's happening?" I demanded of the nurse at the station as I hurried on by. "Wait a minute! You must not go in there!" she called. But I was already in and I saw the nurses and doctor bending over the bed where father lay. Pushing them aside, I looked down at him, and knew instantly that he was gone. "He never woke up to say goodbye," I said sadly, pressing his lifeless hand in mine. "Oh Father, what are we going to do now?"

I rode home in a haze of grief and misery, wondering how I was going to tell mother, but one look at my face as I came in, told her what had happened. She and I sat together trying to think what we had to do, and it was as if we were lost in a fog, and did not know which way to turn. Thankful that the minister of our church arrived to help with arrangements, I began to realize that my plans had to be changed. Not only was there the funeral to see to, mother's future had to be decided, and what about the business? I had no idea what to do, except that I had to send a wire to Travare immediately. I hastily scribbled the message and mother and father's driver took it so I needn't go out. In the wire I only told of father's death and that I would be delayed a week or two, and a letter would follow. I had the wire sent to Charlie, as he was the one on my mind. He would tell Sofie and Luke.

Instead of a week or two, it was nearly four months before matters were cleared up enough for me to leave. I was thankful that things had resolved themselves as well as they had. Mother's widowed sister from Philadelphia had moved to Chicago to live with her. Father's financial manager and I worked out a deal with a competitor who had wanted to acquire the business for some time, but father wouldn't sell. Now I was leaving with quite a sum of money in my name in a bank in Chicago, which was my legacy. Mother had enough capitol also, that she could live on the interest earned very comfortably for the rest of her life. All father's hard work had turned out well for the two of us, and that's how he would have wanted it, but I was so sorry for the bitterness that had been between us last year. I made my mind up then and there, that if I ever had children, I would not drive them away by forcing them into a life they didn't want.

There had been a peculiar silence from Travare the last month and I couldn't help wondering about it. Sofie and Charlie had both written from time to time during the summer telling me of the news, and that they were waiting for me to return, and I hoped they hadn't given up. I had sent a wire telling when my train would arrive, so they would be expecting me.

In the comfortable compartment, I slept deeply and dreamlessly until the conductor rapped on the door to say breakfast was being served. I remembered that first trip, sleeping in the coach and waking all wrinkled and groggy, and afraid to spend even a few cents on breakfast.

My heart grew lighter and lighter as we traveled west through Minnesota. Every familiar landmark was another guidepost on the way home, and I noted each with glee. At last we pulled into Browns Valley station and I was on my feet before the train came to a stop. There was more luggage than when I left, as I had packed more of my things this time. The Travare bus was waiting as usual, but I looked around expecting to see Charlie. However, there was no Charlie, and a little surprised by his absence, I boarded the bus and we headed up the hill.

"Things been goin' on while you been away, Miss," the driver said conversationally, "The commissioners are kinda worried they gonna lose the county seat here." "However could that happen?" I asked in amazement. "It's cause o' Wilmot, they say, but here we are, I'll let Sofie tell you 'bout it. I'll get you unloaded, then I gotta head back with some stuff that's goin' east on the next train." And as we did nearly a year ago, the driver and I piled my boxes and bags on the porch and I went in to find Sofie.

"Am I glad to see ya Margret!" she exclaimed, giving me a hug that nearly broke my ribs. "At least one good thing happened this week." "What on earth is going on Sofie?" I demanded, "And where is Charlie? He said he would be at the station to meet me whenever I came back, and I sent him a wire that I was coming today...But maybe I was just taking too much for granted," I finished rather lamely, feeling foolish. "Oh he woulda been there if he was here, he told me to tell you why he wasn't. Him and Luke and some o' the other commissioners are havin' meetin's out in the county with voters over this trouble with Wilmot." She motioned for me to sit at the table and poured a cup of coffee for me as she always did when I came into her kitchen. "What is the trouble about the county seat? The bus driver started to say something about it, but he said you would tell me the whole story."

So sitting at Sofie's table I heard the story in her words..."Wilmot has got it in their heads that they should have the county seat. I guess they been back and forth to the capitol and finally got leave to put it to a vote. Everbody's up in the air over it. The commissioners been havin' meetin's with as many people as they can. And you should see what's been written' in the papers! Insults flyin' back and forth evry week, it's a disgrace t' snakes, is all I can say. Charlie has to try and stick up for us, so he's been diggin' up dirt about the Wilmot fellas. The elections gonna be purty soon so they have to get around and talk t' folks in the county and try t' get 'em t'vote for us." "Why does Wilmot think they have any more right to it than we do?" I questioned. "They say cause the railroad goes through there it would be better, and that they're easier to get at for the rest o' the county." "But what about this new courthouse? They'll have to build another one over there won't they? The Territory surely wouldn't want that expense." I was thinking out loud as I got up to get more coffee. "I know it!" Sofie exclaimed, "It jest seems so durn dumb to me. I declare, men can sure turn things upside down for everbody. What do you say us women take over, huh? We couldn't do much worse, could we?" She looked at me with the old twinkle in her eye, and got up to finish the dishes.

I sat for a while at the table thinking over what Sofie had told me. The implications of what it would mean for Travare if they lost were grim. This town had been built to BE the county seat. It was true they didn't have the railroad, it was true they were not quite in the center of the county. Browns Valley had both the railroad and access to the lakes for transportation. It would be hard to compete with them this close. Browns Valley had a doctor, bigger stores and more businesses. I shook my head to clear it. This was not the homecoming I had planned, but it was no use to sit and worry, so I got up to help with the dishes.

School started the next week, and my work kept me too busy to concern myself overly much with county problems. Charlie and I had spoken briefly, and his parting words had been that we would have a talk about our future when this mess was taken care of. Every night at the hotel, the talk around the supper table was of the upcoming election, which would be ten days from today, and everyone was nervous and edgy about the outcome.

## CHAPTER 10

I was wondering why the Berger boys had not come back to school, so decided to pay the family a visit the next Saturday. As I approached the house on foot, a large skinny dog barked loudly and barred my path to the door. Luckily Mrs. Berger heard, and came out with a broom and ordered him to be quiet. She stared at me in suspicion and said defensively, "My boys aint done nothin', they ain't even here enymore." I tried to reassure her that I hadn't come to complain about anything, but only to ask if the boys planned to come back to school. "I was hoping they would, Mrs. Berger," I said soothingly, "They were both making very good progress by the end of the term." Which was the truth, they had done well in spite of our unpromising start. Somewhat mollified, Mrs. Berger asked me to come in for a cup of tea.

She pulled a chair up to the table for me and poured a brimming mug from a pot that was stewing over a burner. I braced myself as I took a sip of the bitter brew, then moved a few dirty dishes to make a spot to set it on the cluttered table. "Where are Jonas and Jim?" I asked curiously. "They went west with their Paw to work on the railroad till winter comes." She answered, as she swatted at a fly with a grimy dishrag. "Don't know fer sure when they'll be back. Don't know if they'll be goin' to school either, its up to their Paw. If there's any work to be had for them, he'll be wantin' 'em to work. Their Paw don't hold much with a lot o' schoolin'." "Oh, that's too bad," I said rather hesitantly, "Because, they will need to know reading, writing and figuring numbers to get along in the world these days." "Aw, I dunno, their Paw and me, we never had much schoolin' and we did awright." To that I had no reply, and excusing myself, left the cheerless abode with a sigh of relief. The dog didn't bother me, but I eyed him cautiously as I walked away.

The weather was turning colder now and the leaves were nearly gone from the few trees around the town. Everyone was preparing for winter. Luke had his haystacks moved up by the barn again and was hauling wood from the bottom of the ravines where the floodwaters had brought the logs down the Little Minnesota last spring.

One unusually warm Saturday morning, Charlie came by the hotel early and asked if I would like to take a ride with him down Big Stone

Lake. The boat made the trip up and back nearly every day bringing passengers and freight. Charlie said it wouldn't be long before the lake would be frozen again, and since I had never gone, he thought I might enjoy it. He was right, and I asked him to wait just a couple of minutes while I changed. "Take a warm coat and hat," he warned, "So that we can stay out on the deck and watch the scenery."

We took the hotel bus down to the boat landing so Charlie wouldn't have to leave his horse stand while we were gone. It was a lovely ride down the thirty-five miles to the other end of the lake. There were still some leaves on the few trees and they shone golden and red in the sunlight. The water reflected the blue of the sky, and we leaned over the rail and waved to the people on shore watching us go by.

The boat docked for two hours, and Charlie and I got off and had dinner at a hotel on the shore. I was glad to have this time with him away from the cares of everyday life. We always had plenty to talk about. He enjoyed hearing about my life in Chicago, about my relatives back east and my father's business. I liked to hear about his early life in the Territory, working with the scouts when he was not much more than a boy. He told stories of his fur trading days, when the beaver and otter were plentiful around the lakes. He told me about his parent's deaths in a typhoid epidemic back east and the journey west on his own. Today, while we were eating he told me more of the planning and building of Travare, that he was a part of from the first. Any information about the little town fascinated me, and I soaked up each new bit like a sponge. I would write each piece of information in my diary as I heard it from the townspeople.

Charlie was never afraid to hear my opinions on politics or other issues of the day. He would listen to what I had to say, and if he disagreed, would say so in no uncertain terms, but he always respected what I had to say, unlike the men I had known in Chicago.

Luckily, we heard the whistle of the boat, or we might have missed our ride back, we were so caught up in our conversation, but Charlie grabbed my hand and we ran down to the landing, making it by the skin of our teeth. Laughing like school children, we found two seats on a deserted part of the deck, where we could be out of the wind. "Oh Maggie, we do have a good time together, don't we?" He chuckled pulling my collar closer around my face. The wind was definitely getting colder, and the air smelled like rain. Our good weather was no doubt coming to an end for awhile.

As we sat and watched the Minnesota shoreline going slowly by, I could tell that Charlie had something on his mind, so I just waited, and at last he came out with it. Taking hold of my chair he pulled me closer to him, took my hand in his, and said, "What do you think Maggie, about setting a date right here and now for our wedding? I know I haven't asked you in so many words, but sometimes words are hard for me. You maybe don't believe that with all the talking I do, but I have never asked a woman to marry me before, and hardly know how to begin. I'll just say that I think I fell in love with you the first day I saw you in Sofie's kitchen, all prickly and starchy, spoiling for an argument." At this I had to grin in spite of myself, as I sought for words to answer this man who had been in my thoughts more than any other in my life. "Look at me Margaret!" he finally insisted, when my silence must have lasted too long. Taking my arm and shaking it, he asked impatiently, "Did I wait too long to ask, or is there someone else? I thought you might love me too...was I all wrong?" I sighed as I squeezed his hand and replied, "No Charlie, there is no one else, and yes, I love you too, at least I think so. I know I love being with you, and I love the way you laugh, and the way you look, and I love your blue eyes. But listen to me a minute, I think we should wait to decide anything until all this business with the election has been settled. Tell me, do you ever get the feeling that things are changing, and nothing will ever be like it was?" He stared off into space for awhile and then turned to me with a worried look, "I feel that way every day. I feel that this blasted election none of us asked for, could go either way. Folks seem to be divided pretty evenly about it." He fumbled in his pocket for tobacco and rolled a cigarette absent mindedly while he went on, "But that shouldn't have anything to do with us, we are still going to be here, we will make our home nearby. I'll build a new house, and when you are finished with your school term we can be married." To this I replied, "I just think it would be better not to promise anything at this time. Please, just humor me on this Charlie. Let's wait a few months and see what happens and how we feel when spring comes, then I promise I will give you an answer." I thought I heard him swear under his breath as he struck a match to his cigarette and inhaled deeply. "As much as I hate to agree with you, you might be right, but doggone it, don't think I am not going to hold you to that! Come spring, I will be waiting for you to set the date and that's that!" And he glared at me fiercely. "Yessir, you can count on that, sir," I said meekly with downcast eyes, trying not to laugh. "Margaret! Are you laughing?" he exploded, "Do you want to get thrown overboard right here?" That was too much, and I began to giggle in spite of myself. "Oh dear Charlie, I'm not laughing at you, honestly. Everything has been far too serious lately, that when I see something even remotely funny, like the look in your eyes just then, I can't help myself. Don't you ever have the uncontrollable urge to laugh out loud in church or some other unsuitable place and horrify everyone?" I lay my head on his shoulder and he put his arms around me tightly, as he murmured, "Yes, my sweet, I know what you mean, and that's one of the things I love about you...You want to know something else? Remember the day I took you to see the schoolhouse, the day after you arrived here? When I said one of your jobs would be to light the fire and keep it going? Did you think I didn't guess that you had never done that before? I wanted to laugh then too, at the look in your eyes, but I didn't dare. You would probably have thrown the bucket of coal at me, right?...I would have offered to show you, but didn't want to let on, and I knew you would figure it out somehow." I slapped him on the arm and exclaimed, "Why you miserable wretch! And me worried sick about it. That was the first thing I asked Sofie when we got back, and she was good enough to show me how!" "Oh Maggie, what a pair we are, you and I will have a good time together, mark my words. I can't think of anyone I would rather have sitting with me at the breakfast table in the morning," he chuckled. I smiled, "And I can't think of anyone I would rather have pouring my breakfast coffee, maybe making it too, as you no doubt are better at that than I am!"

By this time, the landing was in sight and we fell silent and just stood by the rail waiting to get off. The realities of the coming week were on our minds as we both looked up the hill to see the lighted windows of Sofie's hotel shining a welcome.

# CHAPTER 11

Monday morning the students and I were back in school as usual, studying the three R.s. For the rest of the town and the commissioners, the election was uppermost in their minds...The presidential race between Cleveland and Blaine took second place to the ongoing battle with Wilmot. "Thank you Lord," I said in my prayers, "That these are peaceful minded men who won't turn to violence." But there was this week's *County Sun* to go to print yet, and I was sure Charlie would pull out all the stops in the contest of insults between the two papers.

I walked back to Sofie's rather later than usual Monday evening, as I had test papers to correct, and was surprised by activity at the courthouse. Usually by this time of day it was locked and dark, and everyone gone. I took a detour to walk past and see what was going on. Charlie was there with the sheriff and his deputy in a serious discussion. Charlie gave me a nod and a smile and motioned that I should wait for him, so I just stood aside out of hearing distance until he was finished.

When Charlie walked over to me, I expected to see the two officers leave also as it was nearly suppertime, but Deputy Chadwick shouldered his rifle and stood guard where he had a good view of all directions. "What in the world is going on?" I asked Charlie in alarm. He took my arm to walk me home and explained that the townspeople were of the opinion that the courthouse should be guarded at night in the event of intruders. "Why? What kind of intruders would break into a courthouse?" I had never heard of such a thing, but Charlie went on to tell of cases, some not very far away, where men had broken in and taken county records. Then they would set up the county seat in their own town. With possession nine tenths of the law, as they say, the one who did the stealing would win. "Why that's illegal!" I sputtered angrily, "How can something done outside of the law stand up in court? I think that sounds ridiculous!" "Now, now, don't get yourself all worked up over nothing," Charlie soothed, "Wilmot might be a bunch of blow hards but I doubt very much they would try anything so foolish, when our courthouse is right here under everyone's nose. But anyway until the election is over we will have a guard posted every night. The sheriff will deputize more of us so we can take turns. We don't want to take any unnecessary risks. There's too much at stake." "Are you still having meetings around the county this week?" I asked him. "I won't be," He replied, "There is too much work getting the paper out this week for me to go, but Harry and Jed will be speaking in two of the townships yet. Then that's it, for campaigning. If we fail, it won't be for lack of trying." He left me at the door with a quick kiss and a smile, and went back to his store building where he would be burning the midnight oil putting his articles together for this week's edition.

The paper came out on Thursday, October 30th. As soon as I got home after school, I grabbed the hotel copy off the hall table to see what Charlie had written. About a third of a column on the front page was devoted to Markham, who was one of Wilmot's main men, and had been slandering the county commissioners in every issue of the *Wilmot Review*. It was a fine comeback, Charlie's article, and I loved it, even though it was disgraceful. He told in detail how Mr.Markham owed all the merchants in Travare and some in Browns Valley, besides which he had left a trail of unpaid debts all the way from Canada, where he originally hailed from.

The first paragraph read: "Wilmot undoubtedly made a mistake when Mr. Markham was chosen as a speaker in the joint discussion. He has not produced one argument. His only words were words of a vile, filthy mouth. He was chosen, doubtless because of blackness, lowness, and lack of self-respect. His tongue knows no language but that of dirt and indecency."

The column to the right of this article was called "Pointers" and it was a long list of reasons to vote for Travare. Down the list were..."Lying has been the stock in trade of the Wilmot Gang. Show by your vote that you did not believe them." And another read..."The Wilmot Gang should take out a patent for the lying machine which they have invented." "Good for you Charlie!" I gloated, still smarting under the uncalled for attack in the *Review* which came out on Tuesday...It had stated that..."Mr. C.B. Preston, who thinks himself such a fine gentleman and so well qualified to run the business of Roberts County, is actually nothing more than a back woodsman who in the not so distant past made his living as a trapper." I had been furious when I read it, but Charlie had laughed loud and long and remarked that at least this once they were not lying.

The last paragraph in the column read, "The taxpayers have built a courthouse at Travare and paid for it. Wilmot wants you to vote to build another. Taxpayers, is that to your interest? We think not." The inside pages of the paper were devoted to national and Territorial news, but I wasn't interested in that tonight and I folded it and went to find Sofie.

Sofie was in the kitchen doing her mending while a delicious smelling kettle of soup bubbled on the back of the stove. I walked over and peeked under the lid and sniffed appreciatively, "Mmmm, venison stew! That's going to hit the spot this chilly night." The pot was full of chunks of meat, onions, carrots and potatoes, and with Sofie's good homemade bread would make a complete meal for the hungry men. Luke was taking his turn standing guard tonight Sofie told me; "So he has to have somethin' hot in his stomach to last him till the next one takes over at 2:00 A.M. I declare to goodness, I'll be so glad when this election bisness is over with so we can get back to normal again. As if Luke don't have enuff t'do without havin' to stand out there with a rifle half the night." But then she confided to me in a low voice, "Say, Margret, jest between you and me, I think these men are enjoyin' this deputy stuff. Probly makes 'em think of the old days when they had to carry a gun 'round wherever they went to keep from getting' et by wild animals." "You might be right, Sofie. It just seems like the men of this world are never satisfied to leave well enough alone. They always have to be stirring things up. Wanting something someone else has...is that it? Think how the world got explored and settled. One kind of people always having to make way for another, down through the centuries"...As I tied on my apron I thought again of the Indians who were giving up their land for money, and what they would do once the money was spent. Would they know how to get along in this new life? I didn't know what the answer was.

# CHAPTER 12

Election morning dawned cold and gray, with a few flakes of snow skittering along the frozen ruts of the streets. There was no school today, and the schoolhouse was being used as the polling place. I had helped Charlie curtain off three corners with blankets yesterday and these would be the voting booths. This morning my stomach was tied in knots with nervousness thinking of the long day ahead before the results would be known. I helped Sofie with breakfast as I usually did on the days when there was no school, and even she had little to say. I watched as she strained the fresh foaming milk Luke had just brought in and when she slopped some over the edge of the pan, she hissed impatiently. "Durn, if I'm not all thumbs today, jest a bundle o' nerves. Couldn't hardly sleep last night for thinkin' what's gonna happen." I knew what she meant, as I had been awake for hours as well, and had wished I could get out of bed and walk the floor. It would have meant disturbing the ones below me, so I lay in bed tossing and turning instead.

I put on my warm coat and shawl and went for a brisk walk over the hills in the afternoon to help pass the time. I looked down at the tiny stream that was the Little Minnesota this time of year. There was ice forming all ready on the edges, and I knew it would not be long before the lakes and sloughs would be frozen solid. The ducks and geese had flown south and the land was quiet as if waiting for whatever winter would bring.

I stayed outside until my feet began to get cold, and at last had no choice but to go inside and get warm. There was a mouth-watering aroma coming from the kitchen, and I went in to see what Sofie was baking today. "Jest a spice cake," she told me, "For dessert tonight while we're sittin' 'round waiting for someone to tell us how it all came out. I'll make a brown sugar frosting to put on. May as well start it now." And she took a pan out of the huge cupboard and measured brown sugar from her barrel. While she stirred in thick cream and set it on the stove to cook, she asked, "What are you are Charlie gonna do? You gettin' married or not? Maybe I'm bein' too nosey, but I can't help wonderin'" I was quiet for a minute before I could think what to say, and finally just told the truth. "He asked me to set a day right away, but I thought it would be better to wait until all this is settled, and he agreed." "Well, jest don't wait too long," she warned, peering at me closely, "He's a good man, and you're not getting' eny younger!" She poked me playfully and chuckled, "I'm jest foolin', you know that, dontcha?" I laughed weakly and replied, "You are right about me not getting any younger. I'm going to be twenty seven next birthday...just about over the hill." "Oh phooey!" she exclaimed, "That don't matter none, don't pay any 'ttention to me. Charlie's no spring chicken either. I'm not sure zactly, but I think he's close to forty." "Thirty-eight, actually," I answered absent-mindedly, as I stirred my cold coffee. "Hey, jest forget I said anything," Sofie said apologetically, "I dint mean to pry, what you two decide is you're own bisness. But if you do get married, can we stand up with ya? Or...wait a minute...maybe you're goin' back to Chicago for the weddin'? I dint even think o' that." "No, I don't think we would be going back to Chicago Sofie, I can't imagine Charlie wanting to do that, nor me either for that matter. Mother could come out here on the train, though. And yes, I would love to have you stand up with me Sofie, I can't think of anyone I would rather have." Sofie beamed happily as she gave the frosting a stir to keep it from sticking to the pan. "A June weddin' would be nice," she said dreamily. "Luke and me was married in February, and the weather freezin' cold. I thought then of a June weddin', but we jest went ahead with it. Had to shovel the sleigh out comin' from the preachers, cause we sunk through a snow drift and jest 'bout tipped over." She shook her head at the memories and murmured, "We had some times, at first. I was purty ignorant, about cookin' and stuff in the house. I had always worked outside cause my folks dint have eny boys. We had some land in Wisconsin cleared, and did some farmin'. Hard work with all the trees to grub out to get a little bit of land. So when Luke and I first talked bout gettin' married, he said he wanted to come out west further where the land was bare. But then we started this place instead, and will jest wait till the reservation opens to get some land t' farm."

It was beginning to get dark by this time, and some of the men would be coming in soon for their supper, so I got the plates and began to set the big table in the dining room. Ben had been out doing the evening chores, and brought in the pails of milk as his father had that morning. He had grown this past year, and was a handsome boy with his father's dark good looks and his mother's sunny smile. Sofie was proud of her boy, and she once confided in me that she "Wished they had a girl too, but their one chick was fine since he was turnin' out so good."

I finally went to bed without having heard any news of how the vote had come out, as it took time to get the word from all over the county. In the morning, however, the message had gotten through that we had won! But there was a rather large fly in the ointment, as Wilmot was demanding a recount. It seems that if the votes would have all qualified, Wilmot would have won. But two townships in the Wilmot area were thrown out because of technicalities. There was some confusion with the number of voters in one township and in the other, a member of the election board had taken the ballot box home with him at lunchtime. "Well! Why do they get a recount, when that was illegal?" I wanted to know. "I don't know," Charlie said wearily, "But they got it, and now we have to wait again to know where we stand." He looked so tired, my heart went out to him, as he sat slumped with his elbow on the dining room table. "How long do you think that will take?" I asked. "It will be days before we hear anything I think," he answered. "But now I am going home for an hour's nap before doing anything else, I'm done in." He pushed back his chair and got to his feet. As he passed me, he whispered, "Chin up Maggie, don't worry so, let's see one of those smiles." He grinned at me in his old way as he walked down the hall and out the front door.

# CHAPTER 13

The days passed somehow. I was back at my teacher's desk, the pupils back in theirs. Jonas and Jim Berger had not come to school yet, and deep down I was relieved although I felt guilty to admit it even to myself. The other children were well behaved and doing quite well, and we had an orderly schoolroom. I had a talk with the school board before the term had started and requested that I be allowed to live at the hotel and pay for my own room and board. They had agreed that it made sense as long as I could afford it, since the school was fairly close to the edge of town. The board had made good their promise of more books, and the children and I were making use of them everyday. We now had some recent geography books with up to date maps, and a few reference books, besides new readers for most of the grades.

At last the day came when a jubilant group of men came storming in with the news that Travare had won the recount! It seemed they had stopped off at the saloon in Browns Valley for a few celebration drinks on their way. Laughing and talking at the top of their voices they sat around the table at the hotel until Sofie told them in no uncertain terms to clear out. Charlie and Luke were two of the few who weren't drinking, and the four of us sat in the kitchen quietly enjoying the feeling of victory together.

That night I had the first sound sleep of weeks, as must have many other Travare residents, because when daylight came, someone made the ghastly discovery that the courthouse had been robbed sometime during the early morning hours. No longer seeing any need for it, the men had not been on guard, and after consuming great quantities of liquor had been sleeping the sleep of the dead. When the alarm went out, the town sprang into action and sleighs set out to follow the tracks. But of course they led straight to Wilmot across country, and soon they turned back when realizing the certainty of what had happened. Racing to town, the commissioners gathered to decide what course of action to take, but missing their chairman, they came to the hotel to inquire if we had seen Charlie. No one had since last night, and fearing foul play they began to search. He was found at last...in a corner of the stable in back of his store building tied hand and foot with a gag in his mouth.

So then we had the full story of what had happened. Charlie had been starting out in the early morning hours as he usually did to pick up the mail, when he heard horses coming. He turned back to see what was going on and was spotted by the lookouts. To prevent him from getting away and calling for help, he was bound and gagged while they carried out the safes with all the papers and records.

I hovered anxiously in the background while the men milled around in total disarray. The old line "Defeat snatched from the jaws of victory," came to mind, as I thought of the happiness of last night. Feeling a headache coming on I left the room and went to get ready for school. "If this ain't th' limit!" Was the way Sofie put it, as she slammed things around in the kitchen. "If them men had been tendin' t'bisness last night instead of guzzlin' booze, this wouldn't have happened! They shoulda known them Wilmot fellas would try somethin' crooked!" She banged the iron frying pan so hard onto the stove lid that it made my head hurt worse than ever. I was beyond words, so just took my coffee mug and went slowly up the stairs to my room. I sat looking out the window at the beautiful courthouse, now useless to all intents. Once records were stolen, Charlie had told me, it was practically impossible to get them returned unless by order of the courts.

I quietly let myself out and walked to the schoolhouse to start the fire. Needing time to collect my self, I was thankful for the hour before the children would begin arriving. They had of course heard something had happened by the time they came to school, and began asking me to explain it right away. I told them truthfully that I couldn't answer their questions and we would all just have to wait and see what happened next. In the meantime, we would keep on with our studies, and do the best we could.

## Chapter 14

The weeks went by with the commissioners struggling to carry on as if they were still the heads of the county. The lawyers were studying the law, trying to figure the next moves. Christmas came and went without many festivities. We went to church on Christmas Eve, Charlie and I, Luke, Sofie, and Ben. The tiny Episcopal Church was full and it was a lovely service. It lifted all our spirits, and as we rode back in the sleigh Charlie put his arm around me and put a tiny package in my mittened hand. "Just keep it for now," he whispered, "And in spring when this is over, we will set our date, then I will put it on your finger." He smiled down at me in the moonlight, and pulled me closer. "It will be all right Maggie, I'm sure it will. We are working on an idea that might turn things around for us." "What is it? Or can't you say?" I asked. "No, better not," He replied. "The fewer people who know about it, the better. It's nothing illegal or dangerous," he hurried to explain, when he saw my skeptical look. "You'll know soon enough. In a few weeks we will have something to send up to Bismarck and that's all I can say. Now put your curious mind to rest and think about me instead, all right?"

Mother sent a large Christmas package of goodies from one of the specialty shops where she had always bought gifts. Creamy yellow cheeses, bottles of wine, chocolates of all kinds. I shared them on New Years Eve as the five of us waited for the new year...We played games and sat around the parlor fire till the clock struck twelve, and wished each other a happy year for 1885.

The winter settled in with the usual icy cold winds that blew off the lakes and plenty snow. Many mornings I plodded through knee high drifts breaking a path to the school, my skirts dragging. I pulled them along behind me and wished to wear trousers like a man. Why do women have to be cursed with such awkward clothing, I wondered? Once Charlie took me ice skating on Lake Traverse on a fine Saturday afternoon. We took his sleigh with Little Bird stepping daintily along. She would toss her head like she enjoyed hearing the bells jingle that were attached to her harness.

Charlie was usually too busy for us to spend time together, but I didn't mind. I had plenty of reading and studying to do. I had been gathering information about the Agency School, as it interested me very much. It wouldn't be possible for me to ever work there if we continued to live in Travare, as it was much too far away. Charlie would never consider living anywhere else I was sure, but I could still read how it operated. I had written down some of the Dakotah words the way they sounded as Charlie taught them to me. Whenever I had a chance, I would coax him to teach me some more. I had made a little progress, but it was hard going without a written dictionary. I wanted to be able to converse with some of the older people in their language and learn as much of their tribe's history as I could.

About a month later, Charlie told us what the commissioner's plan had been. It was time to send county warrants to Bismarck for the legislature to approve and allot the money for their payment. He said at the very bottom, the men had inserted a line that declared Travare to be the official Roberts County Seat. "It should work," he said, "And Lawyer Barnes told us its perfectly legal to do that." "Mercy!" Sofie exclaimed, "I never heard o' sech a thing, seems kinda sneaky, but if it works, that would be the end of our troubles wouldn't it?" "Yes, that should do it," Charlie agreed, "Then Wilmot will be forced to return the records and things will be like they were before. Now, all we have to do is wait again, and try to be patient."

At about the same time the first Mayflowers were seen on the hillsides, the news came down from Bismarck. The warrants were paid and the line at the end of the page had been passed into law. There was just one large difference...some Wilmot people had gotten wind of the plan and somehow changed the wording from Travare to Wilmot. Charlie told us what happened as soon as they got word, and I wanted to cry, or scream, at the unfairness of it all. But I just sat like a stone staring into his eyes that were clouded with defeat, and only wished there was something I could do to take that look away. But there was nothing. Their plan had failed, and this was the end. Now the commissioners had to meet with the townspeople to try to explain it.

The word was passed that there would be a meeting that night at the courtroom, and by seven o' clock the room was full. From the looks on most faces it was obvious they all ready knew the news was not good. When Charlie told them what Wilmot had done to change the wording on the bill, an angry buzz broke out all over the room. One man stood up and shouted, "I say we get our rifles and go over there and steal those records back. Come on men, we aren't going to take this lying down, are we?" There were other voices in agreement and the buzz turned into an angry roar. Finally Charlie rapped with the judge's gavel until the noise died, then he said, "No one is going to do anything of the kind! We will have the sheriff and deputy collect all your firearms and lock them up, if you don't stop talking like this. We are not going to have someone shot or men put in prison trying anything so foolish. We lost...and that's all there is to it. It's over...Now we have to decide if we are going to hold our town together or let it fall apart because of this. We all still have our businesses, the school, and the flourmill plans are going ahead, so there will be more jobs. So let's just forget about this and get on with our work. It's all we can do now. We did our best, and we failed, and that's it."With that he stood up to leave and the other commissioners followed him, so the crowd had no choice but to disperse.

  Three more weeks went by, and the Mayflowers were replaced with yellow buttercups scattered through the grass. On the surface nothing seemed much different except the empty courthouse. There were rumors though, of other changes coming. One morning some men from Bismarck had come to look the courthouse over. They had walked all around it and through it, then had a long discussion among themselves. Charlie told me about it that afternoon. The plan was to move it to Wilmot when the roads got drier they had said. "Move it?" I exclaimed in disbelief, "How in the world do you move a big building like that?" "There's ways to do it," Charlie answered, "So long as the ground is solid, and they have enough power to pull it." Then he jumped up, and pulled me with him, "Come for a buggy ride with me Maggie...I want to talk to you in private...Get your bonnet and I'll hitch up Little Bird...hurry now...I'll be back in a minute!"

  We drove west away from town on the trail that continued from Main Street. Then the road curved to the south and he slowed Little Bird to a walk. When he found a place to pull over onto the grass he stopped and tied the reins. "Look at those hills tonight Maggie, aren't they a pretty sight?" "Yes, they are. It's so clear you can see for miles. It's so beautiful here Charlie, I don't know how any place could be better." I answered. But he was quiet for so long that I finally had to look at him to see what he was thinking. He turned to me then, and quickly said, "Margaret, I'm thinking of moving on further west, probably Montana. I know I said I was staying in spite of everything, but now I can see what's going to happen here. Travare is going to fizzle out completely, or I miss my guess. Lawyer Barnes is going to the Valley. The drug store plans to move their business to Wilmot, and there are one or two others talking about clearing out." "But that's terrible!" I cried in anger, "Moving to Wilmot! That's practically treason!" "But it's not, my darling Maggie, it's not an enemy country, it's our county seat. They have a right to go where they think they will do better. But listen to me now, this is important. Would you be willing to marry me and go where we can find a place to start all over again? I don't think I can stand staying here and watching as everything we worked for comes to an end. I've been talking to the editor in the Valley, and he would buy out the *Sun* and combine it with his and make a new paper. Matt Brewer would take over the mail, and my store...that's nothing to worry about. I haven't been stocking up lately, just have to clean it out. Take some with us, and let Sofie have the rest." As he talked on, my mind was racing in panic...Montana! How could I go to Montana? What was he thinking of? I was all ready to stay here in Dakota Territory the rest of my life because of him, and now he tells me he's going to Montana. I couldn't take it in, and turned to him in bewilderment when he finally stopped talking. "Charlie...I can't possibly go to Montana. What about the school? What about your plans to build a house here?" "I know, I know," he said unhappily, "But I thought you might understand that I can't stay. School will be out in another couple weeks, and then there's nothing to stop us. I'll build you a house out west. There's plenty of trees in the mountains to build with, not like here." He was rambling again, and I had to stop him and make him see sense. "Charlie, now please listen to me. I am not the wife you need to go into the wild country. How could I be any help to you? I barely know how to cook and light a fire in a stove, never mind a campfire. I would be a hindrance to you, and would hate that. Besides, I shouldn't go so far away from my mother. Here at least I can hop on the train and be back in Chicago in no time if she needed me. I know that sounds odd when I couldn't wait to get away from there, but I am the only child she has." Now I was the one rambling on, and I knew it, so at last my words just dwindled to nothing, and I sat and stared miserably at the setting sun.

Charlie reached for my hands and raised them to his lips, and I was sure there was a glisten of tears in his eyes as he said sadly, "I would take you with me if you didn't know how to do a blessed thing to help. But I can't argue with you about going far away from your mother. There wouldn't be any way to communicate except by mail and that could take weeks. Getting back would be a long journey that's for sure. It's been many years since I lost my folks, and I wasn't even considering your feelings about that. I'm sorry Maggie. But drat it all, I'm sorrier for myself! I don't want to lose you. Let's leave it for a day or two...you think it over...I know I sprung this on you too suddenly.

Please, just don't say no right now, give yourself a few days and see how you feel then, all right? Let's say Saturday, we'll talk again and then you give me an answer?" What could I do but agree, but I knew my answer wouldn't change, even though it broke my heart.

## CHAPTER 15

How I got through the next days I really never knew afterwards. I must have taught my classes, eaten meals, combed my hair, done all the endless things that make up a day, and no one guessed. Not even Sofie knew I walked in a haze of pain, as I agonized over and over what to do. How could I let him go without me? Why wouldn't he stay? My mind went round and round until I thought I should go insane and end up in one of those dreadful asylums. "Pull yourself together!" I finally said to myself in anger Saturday evening, as I knew Charlie would be coming to hear my decision. Slowly I opened the top dresser drawer and took out the tiny box that was tucked away back in the corner. Sitting on the bed I looked one last time at the lovely little ring inside. A handmade silver band set with turquoise stones and Indian carving all around it. He told me it had been made by a friend of his who lived a long way west of the Missouri. I had thought it the most beautiful ring I had ever seen, and now would never wear it.

I sat there until Sofie called up the stairs that Charlie was here to get me, then got my shawl out of the closet and walked slowly down. He looked at me steadily as I came toward him and the answer must have been plain to see in my face, as he said nothing, just opened the door and helped me into the buggy.

This time we drove north down the hill toward the Valley and stopped beside the river. The moon was out and it was a warm spring evening, but my skin was cold and clammy like I was coming down with fever and ague. I knew it wasn't sickness of body, but of heart, and if this was how love made one feel, I swore to myself...Never again!

At last with a sigh Charlie turned to me and said softly, "Well Maggie?" In answer I handed him the ring box wordlessly and shook my head. He didn't take it but just kept staring into my eyes in the twilight. "What are you going to do? I feel responsible for your coming out here and I don't want to just leave not knowing you'll be all right." I managed a smile then as I looked into those blue eyes, "I will be fine Charlie, don't worry. You go ahead. I'm sure Montana will be wonderful. And me? I think I will keep on teaching for awhile yet. I may apply at the Agency School. I believe I would like to work with the

Indian children for a term or two and see how that goes. I heard they are always short of staff there." He scowled down at me then, "I don't want to go without you, really I don't. I think we would make a great team and you would learn to love Montana. Think of the mountains...and the rivers full of fish. There might even still be beaver out there, who knows?" He looked at me with a trace of his old spirit and then I knew...Charlie Preston would be fine, with or without Margaret Sinclair as his wife. After all he was the boy who came out west at sixteen and made a life in Indian country. He would find a dream again, I was sure of it. And I would survive too. Somehow I would get through this and find my world in teaching as I had once before.

Neither of us had anymore to say as we drove back to the hotel. As we stopped at the porch I remembered the ring that was still clutched in my hand and reached again to give it to him. He took my hand and closed it saying, "You keep it Maggie, I don't want it back. It was made just for you. Wear it anyway, and think of me sometimes when you see it on your finger." I tried to tell him again how sorry I was, but he just shushed me and pulled me close. "I'll never forget you Maggie, but I want you to be happy. When I'm gone, don't get all bogged down with regrets. You go on and do what you want. Teach those kids at the Agency if that is your dream. I'm sure you will be great at it. I wish I would be here to finish teaching you the language, but there are others who will. Ask Sam. He'd be glad to help you with it." I looked up at him in shock, "Why? Are you leaving all that soon?" He let me go then and looked out across the hill to the moon shining on the sliver of lake. "I intended to wait until early summer, but everything here is pretty much taken care of so there is nothing to wait for now, I guess."

I stumbled a little as he held the door for me and asked uncertainly, "Will you come around to say goodbye before you leave?" He didn't meet my eye as he replied, "I can be gone by first light, if I get busy and pack up tonight. I'll be traveling pretty light anyway since it'll just be me." He looked at me then and said softly, "I hate good-byes. I would rather just leave you here and say, "See you soon Maggie." And with that he was gone. "See you soon Charlie," I whispered, and went in and closed the door.

I intended to creep up to my room and wallow in despair, but Sofie waylaid me before I got to the stairs to ask if I had supper. She peered closely at my red eyes and demanded, "Alright ya fool woman! He asked ya to go with him and you said NO, din't ya? The best catch in the whole county and ya let him get away...Oh! I just don't understand it!" And she gazed at me in exasperation with hands on her hips. Sofie had never talked to me like this before and all of a sudden I was reminded of father scolding because I was never satisfied with any of the young men back home. Stifling a hysterical giggle, I sat down with a thump on one of the kitchen chairs. "Sofie, you are absolutely right. I guess I am an idiot for turning down a man half the women in the county would give their eyeteeth for. But I can't leave everything and go to Montana, I just can't. I'm never going to look sideways at another man in my whole life, it hurts too much to fall in love." But Sofie wasn't through with me yet because she retorted, "Hog wash! I jest know some sweet talkin' worthless drifter'll come along and you'll fall for him like a ton o' bricks. Then you'll probly foller him to the North Pole, pullin' his dog sled! I always thought you and Charlie were the perfeck couple right from the first. I feel plumb awful 'bout this. Oh my! I jest 'membered...no June weddin.'" The sad look on her face made me feel worse than ever and I got up and put my arms around her. "Sofie, I promise you I will never fall for a sweet talking worthless drifter, but if you see me doing something so foolish, just hit me over the head with your rolling pin...Please!"At this we both had to laugh a little, and she must have forgiven me because she got busy and made us both a cup of cocoa, her sure cure for bad days.

Sleep wouldn't come that night until dawn was breaking, and when I finally awoke, I called down to tell Sofie not to wait for me for church. I spent most of the morning in my room wondering about my life and if I had made an awful mistake. Then Charlie's words came back to me..."Don't get bogged down in regrets." Remembering that helped me get dressed and face the day. I even felt hungry enough to rummage around in Sofie's cupboard for some bread and jam. Taking my breakfast and a warmed up mug of coffee, I went out on the porch to see what the weather was like. It was a lovely morning, all blue skies and blue water in the distance, the grass thick and green on the hillsides. There was a meadowlark singing somewhere nearby, and Luke's cows were grazing out in the pasture.

While sitting on the step, I thought I heard the snuffling whicker of a horse nearby and walked around the side of the hotel to investigate. My heart gave a jump as I saw Little Bird tied by Luke's barn. My first thought was, "He didn't leave after all!" But then I saw a clumsily tied bow made of twine around her neck with a piece of paper attached. It was folded in half with my name on the outside. Taking it off carefully so as not to tear it, I read what he had written while tears ran unheeded down my face. "My dearest Maggie, I want you to have

Little Bird for your own. She and I have been over many trails together, but the one to Montana might be too hard for her. I know you will take good care of her, and she will do the same for you. I had a small saddle that was hardly used, and left it in Luke's barn. It should fit you all right. It's not a sidesaddle, so you will have to ride like a scandalous modern woman! Take her out every day if you can so she doesn't get too fat. Think of me sometimes. Me-YEH chon-t'kin-yah ne-YEH...Have you learned these words yet? C.P."

As I leaned against the mare's smooth neck, all the confusion of the last months washed over me, and I wept for all of us...Charlie and me, the lost courthouse and fading town, the other friends that were moving away...my father, who I would never see again in this life...It felt like the weight of the world had fallen on me. I don't know how long I stood there with my tears washing Little Bird's coat, but at last she grew restless and rubbed my arm with her nose for some attention. I scratched her ears as I wiped tears on my sleeve, and talked to her softly. "You're going to miss him too, aren't you old girl? So we'll just have to stick together and make the best of it. We'll be all right. You just stay here for now, and later you and I are going for a long ride. We'll ride over the hills and look at the lakes, maybe even ride out to visit some friends. I haven't seen Lars and Inga for awhile." I kept on talking to her while she grazed on the new grass until I felt a little better. Going back to the porch, I saw the cup sitting there. The coffee was cold, so I gave it a toss over the railing and with a last look at the glorious day, went inside to get some more.

# CHAPTER 16

April, 1896...The Mayflowers were blooming again when I pulled on the reins and turned the buggy onto the grassy hilltop overlooking the Valley. It was a pilgrimage of sorts that brought me to the exact spot where Charlie and I had sat that long ago day of the school picnic. Spring of '84, my first spring in Dakota Territory, the first term of school over, the first time I had ever heard a meadowlark sing or seen the Mayflowers that bloomed on the hills. It was the first time too; that Charlie had held my hand and I had looked into those blue eyes and felt for the first time that I might have found a man I could love.

Years had passed since I left Travare and went to work at the Government School in Goodwill Township. We never came this way anymore to get on the train. Now we board at Sisseton, just four miles from my house. Sisseton, through Keller, Wilmot, Corona, and Milbank, then on to Minneapolis and Chicago. Mother had been out to see me a few times, not staying long...She couldn't understand my way of life, and after a week or two was ready to go back to her own. She didn't entertain much anymore but still enjoyed her afternoon visits and charities. We were satisfied to see one another once a year, as we each knew the other was content.

Looking east, the foundation of the courthouse was still plain to see. Other buildings had been moved away as well. Charlie's store, which had also been the postoffice, was gone. Probably to a farm somewhere in the township. A few houses still stood below the hill by the river where the flourmill had been. That too was gone...burned to the ground one windy night in June of '92. That was the final nail in the coffin of Travare...The hotel building still stands, now a private home, so there is one thing familiar to see at least. How could a town disappear this fast? I wondered again for the hundredth time what could have been done differently. Even without the courthouse, why did everyone give up? After one more term, it was decided to close the school near the townsite and combine the children who were left with one of the schools further out in the country. So then I was free to look for a job elsewhere.

My horse began to move restlessly and I crooned softly to her as I climbed back into the buggy. She was as beautiful as her mother,

Little Bird, and had the same good nature. She took me everywhere I needed to go around the neighborhood, but this was the longest drive we had taken, just the two of us. I wanted to come here to think and remember...and once more make a decision about my life.

I married, almost to the word, of what Sofie had predicted..."A sweet talkin' worthless drifter." I still blushed in shame when thinking how gullible I had been. I would listen to no one. Not even Sofie, who tartly reminded me of what I said that night about her rolling pin. And all because of his blue eyes that reminded me so much of Charlie. There I said it. All these years I would never admit it even to myself. Anyway, Sofie would have nothing to do with the wedding and I had to have someone else stand up with me the day we were married. Harry wasn't totally worthless, he was a salesman, and a good one, I'll give him that. We were married three years before he ran off with the wife of one of his customers. He took with him a sizable chunk of my inheritance that had been transferred from Chicago to the Bank of Sisseton.

After waiting two years I filed a divorce petition on the grounds of desertion. The worst of it was we never had a child. The children at the school filled the gap somewhat. Some of them even spent weeks at a time with me while their parents were gone hunting for the winter. I smiled to myself thinking of the children...the hundreds who had been through my classrooms. They had made my life worthwhile, and I hoped that to them I had been an influence for good. Sofie and Luke's Ben had become a teacher and was working at the school in Corona. Sofie had confided one day that he had said Miss Sinclair was the reason he had gone on to school and taken up teaching himself.

Sofie and Luke had gotten the homestead they wanted when the reservation opened in '92. The land lay in the valley east of the hills. It had a creek running through and good flat fields to farm. They were doing well, both working hard as ever. They were eight miles away, but I could drive over there now and then to visit. Sometimes I would take one or two of the children from school so they could see the baby lambs and calves.

The problem on my mind today was that I had been asked to marry, by a widower from the neighborhood, whose wife had died of the fever two years ago. He had three school age children, two girls and a curly haired little boy, who he was raising alone. He had begun calling on me four months ago, and I suspected his intentions were serious when he started asking questions about my former husband. "No," I told him, "Harry is not coming back, and if he did, I wouldn't have him on a silver platter with an apple in his mouth." It was supposed to be a joke, but Marcus just looked at me blankly and changed the subject. Since then I had gotten word of Harry's death by the hand of an irate husband somewhere in New York State, so it was no longer a question anyway.

It bothered me more than a little that Marcus had no sense of humor. At first I thought it was the tragedy of losing his wife that made him so serious, but at last I realized that was how he was and always would be. It didn't seem right to let such a thing as not being able to laugh much bother me. I did have to wonder though what he would think when one of my giggling attacks hit me at the wrong time as was bound to happen eventually. I was sure he would not be amused. He had also stated in no uncertain terms, that "After we are married you won't be working out anymore, as I am well able to provide for us." I didn't care for that attitude, as I had not been totally cared for by a man since leaving my father's house. Even married to Harry I hadn't had the feeling of being under his thumb, as he was away on his rounds much of the time. I had been able to keep on teaching, though it was technically against the rules for a married woman to be hired. They bent the rule in my case however, since I was well qualified and knew the language fairly well and as usual they were short staffed.

The sun was low over the hills by the time I reached home, and I still had not made a decision about Marcus. It would have to wait until tomorrow, because now I had to unharness Buttercup......rub her down and put her in the stable with a feeding of oats and water. On my way to the house I sighed, and thought how pleasant it would be to have someone waiting for me, but the windows were dark, and I would be having supper alone as usual.

# Chapter 17

School had been dismissed for a short vacation, the children were gone with their families, and I was trying to hoe up a tiny spot of rock hard earth to plant a few vegetables. In aggravation, I chopped until my face was dripping with sweat, determined this contrary piece of ground was not going to defeat me. So intent was I on my work that I didn't hear anyone ride up until a familiar voice asked, "Need some help with that Maggie?" As if in a dream, I looked up to see Charlie sitting astride a shining black horse, just as I had pictured him returning many times in the years of his absence. Taking off my hat I wiped my face on my apron thinking wildly of how terrible I looked, and only wanting to turn and run. Slowly he dismounted and walked over to me and then I could see the lines in his face and the gray in his hair. But the eyes were the same...Oh my heaven, just the same. Looking away finally, I noticed for the first time another rider just behind the black stallion. Pulling myself together, I managed to smile and say weakly, "Hello Charlie, how are you?" Not..."Charlie, where have you been for eleven years? I missed you so badly...I made a huge mistake...why didn't you make me go with you? I was terribly stupid and now it's too late..." I said none of these things, but only asked politely, "Would you and your friend care to come in? I'll make some lemonade, you must be thirsty. It's very warm today, I do believe summer is here to stay." Going on about the weather of all things, I thought in disgust, after eleven years, talking about the weather. "Thanks Maggie," Charlie replied, "That would be wonderful, but if we could water our horses first please?" He handed the reins to the young Indian boy who rode the other pony and he led them away to the well while Charlie came in with me.

As I hung my hat on the hook, I asked how he knew where to find me and he mentioned they had been at Luke and Sofie's place. "I suppose Sofie couldn't wait to tell you I am divorced?" I blurted out. "Well it did come up in the conversation before I left," he replied, as he shifted nervously from foot to foot. I motioned for him to sit at the kitchen table while I made the lemonade, but he wandered off into the sitting room, looking at pictures absently, picking the handmade gifts from my school children off the whatnot and putting them back...Running his fingers over the keys of the piano. I watched him silently as it was obvious there was something on his mind that he was trying to put into words. At last he came back to the kitchen and stood uneasily by the door, as if prepared for flight. "Charlie," I ventured at last, "What is wrong with you? Why are you so quiet and jumpy? Are you running from the law, or what? For heaven's sake, say what's on your mind...it can't be that terrible can it?" I tried to keep a light tone, but it didn't work very well, and I ended with a squeak.

At last then he began to talk..."Maggie," he said, looking at me carefully, "That boy out there...Jonathan...is my son. I brought him back to go to school. I've heard good things about your school here at the Agency, even all the way out west. He needs to learn things I can't teach him." With that said, he sat on a chair by the table, and continued to watch me warily. I knew he had said other words but my brain wouldn't take them in. It had gotten stuck on the ones..."That boy out there is my son." A son?...Charlie had a son?...Some other woman had his son? The words kept running around and around in my head until sanity began to return, and I wondered what was the matter with me anyway? Had I expected him to live alone forever when I had refused him? "His mother?"...I asked hesitantly. "Dead." He answered shortly. "Diphtheria, most of her family wiped out in two weeks, and nothing or no one to help. Jonathan was only a baby then and somehow...by a miracle I guess, he and I didn't get it. We have been alone since. I took him everywhere with me. Carried him on my back like his mother did." I looked at him in shock. "How could you care for a baby? I can't imagine it...why didn't you come back with him? You would have had help here from your friends...didn't you think of that?" "Of course I thought of it!" he answered angrily. "But how could I come crawling back admitting I couldn't handle things myself after all my big talk of going west and starting over. And with a half Indian baby besides...not many of my friends would have taken kindly to that! I doubt you would have either, Maggie. Anyway, once he got a little older it became easier, when he could walk or ride in the saddle with me." "Oh Charlie," I said sadly, "What a pair we have been. If I hadn't been so afraid of living in the wilds, and of taking a chance with you, he could have been my son." I was throwing pride to the winds by saying such a thing. But I was beyond caring about pride, as I gazed at the face that had haunted my dreams for eleven years. He looked back at me cautiously as if not quite believing what he was hearing, and began to reply, but just then there was a tap at the door as Jonathan waited to be asked in.

I jumped up quickly and opened the door, realizing the lemonade had not been started. Working with the squeezer and lemons I glanced up now and then to watch Charlie as he spoke softly to his son. The love in both faces was plain to see, and I envied them. Jonathan was tall for his age. His dark hair had been cut with a hunting knife from the looks of it but his eyes were bright with intelligence. Startled by his eyes, I looked closer, and sure enough...they were blue, not brown as I had first thought. While I poured the lemonade I asked where they had been staying, thinking, probably with Sofie and Luke. But Jonathan spoke up and replied. "We just make camp and sleep under the stars like we did on the trail. We can sleep most anyplace, can't we Father?" "Yes son," Charlie answered fondly, "I guess we have slept outside more than inside during our time together except for winters. And Maggie, if you think Dakota winters are cold, try the Montana mountains in January!"

"Tell me about it, please, I want to hear what it is like. Was it as beautiful as you thought? Were the rivers full of fish and beaver really?" Charlie grinned at me, almost in his old way and replied, "Yes to both. It is a wonderful land, unspoiled yet by too many people. The rivers are so clear you can see the fish...bears come to the riverbanks and scoop them up. The woods are full of deer; we were never without meat. And the trees! You could build a cabin from trees that were cut within just a few feet, they are so thick. Of course if you want to plant some corn or beans, it's a job clearing." "Like Wisconsin?" I asked curiously, remembering what Sofie had said about grubbing trees out to plant crops. "Not exactly." He laughed, "Those hills out west are a lot higher and so are the trees...tall, tall trees. So different from Dakota Territory. I guess every part of the country has its special things, but where home is always seems the best." Home...Did he still think of home here? Or did he mean home was Montana? I had assumed he meant to put Jonathan in the boarding school and leave again. but didn't want to ask...not yet.

When the lemonade was drunk to the last drop, Charlie asked Jonathan if he would like to go out and look around for awhile while he had a talk with his old friend Maggie. The boy rose obediently and disappeared like a shadow out the door. I noticed he was wearing deerskin moccasins, and he moved with the fluid grace common to the Indian men and boys. Now that we were alone, I was struck with a rare attack of shyness, remembering my outburst, and to cover it, jumped up to clear the glasses from the table. But before I could pick up the first one Charlie's arm had reached out and caught mine, as he said softly, "Sit Maggie...sit and talk to me. You know about my life...now tell me what went wrong with yours." I chewed my lip nervously and muttered, "I thought you said Sofie told you about it." "She did, but I want to hear it from you, because maybe Sofie was just giving me her one sided opinion of your...husband. I never wanted you to be unhappy, you know that, so why did you go and marry a 'no 'count scoundrel?'"

At that I had to laugh, "All right! I know those are Sofie's words. She nearly disowned me over marrying Harry, as she must have seen things about him that I didn't, or didn't want to. He wasn't the man I thought he was and after three years he decided he wanted someone else...and I guess I didn't care enough to make him want to stay." I wasn't about to disclose what I had only admitted recently about my real reason for noticing Harry in the first place.

"So now...what about the sober, steady widower who has asked for your hand despite the scandal of your divorce? Looking for a mother for his children and a housekeeper, I take it." Really, this was too much. In anger I jumped up and faced him across the table, "How dare you question me like this Charles Preston! Marcus is a fine man. He's a successful farmer, a good father, and a deacon of the Church, respected in the community...I should be proud to be his wife." To which Charlie retorted, "In that case why is it taking so long for you to give this paragon of virtue your answer?" If this wasn't the last straw. "What is going on? Does Sofie Johnson have spies out watching my every move?" I slumped in the chair again and rubbed my forehead that was now beginning to ache on top of everything else. Finally I answered honestly, "I don't know why I haven't told him yes or no yet. Just don't want to make yet another mistake, I suppose. It would be a comfortable life, I would love his children, and learn to care for him in time I'm sure, but I just don't know. I think I'm too old to marry again anyway." To which he replied chuckling, "Yes, I think you are much too far over the hill Maggie, if I were you I would not even consider it."

As he arose and walked out the door calling for Jonathan, I couldn't help smiling to myself. He had not changed at all in spite of a few gray hairs and some age lines. He still had that same wicked sense of humor. But what was he thinking of...quizzing me like that about my intentions...did my plans really matter to him?

I walked out to the stable while they were untying the horses, and that's when Charlie noticed Buttercup. "Well, well, who have we here?" He asked softly. "Little Bird's, or I miss my guess." "Yes," I answered proudly, "She's Little Bird's last colt. I was almost afraid that she was too old after not foaling for years, but I did want to have a descendant of hers when she would be gone. She delivered beautifully though, and lived to see her baby grown. It was a year this past winter I had her put down. She had something wrong with her insides, and was in such pain. I just couldn't let her go on like that." Charlie rubbed her neck gently, and Buttercup glanced at him curiously once, before going back to munching her hay. The faraway look on his face told me he was remembering the times past with Little Bird, riding the hills along the lakes, bringing the mail up to Travare, sleigh rides down the hill into the Valley.

"I never got to thank you for giving her to me," I told him quietly, "You'll never know how much that meant to have her for company after you left. Little Bird helped me get through the hard days of seeing the courthouse moved away, and all the other changes." "I'm glad if she made things easier for you," he answered. "It was one of the things that made it possible for me to keep going, thinking of you two together."

He was looking out over the hills now that were turning purple in the late afternoon sun. "I didn't realize it before, but you are almost in the foot hills, It's beautiful, isn't it?" "I like it here," I agreed, "It's home now. At first I didn't think I would like anywhere as well as the hills of Travare...looking down on Browns Valley. Have you been there yet?" I asked it hesitantly, not wanting to open any more old wounds. "No, I haven't gotten that far yet, but Luke said there's not much to see anymore. I guess nearly everything has been moved away. Someday it will probably all be plowed fields and no one will even remember," he finished sadly. "I was there not long ago," I told him, "And I think there will always be someone who will recall Travare. After all why wouldn't folks want to know that it was the very first county seat of Roberts County?" "I hope so," he said, "But what were you doing all the way over there?" he asked. "Just remembering," I answered quietly, not wanting to say anymore about it. Then he went on, "You know, It seemed like the end of the world to me when it all fell apart, but since then I've realized there are more important things in life." As he spoke, his gaze went to Jonathan who was waiting patiently for him outside. "He's a good boy, and I want him to be educated, so that he amounts to something more than I did," he said determinedly. "What are you talking about?" I objected, "How can you say such a thing? You were the smartest man in Travare, the one who did most of the planning, and who worked the hardest before the election but you?"

"Maybe I was something then," he murmured, "but now I just feel like a has been. A has been commissioner, a has been storekeeper and newspaperman, even a has been fur trader." But then he had to laugh in spite of himself, "Listen to me, I don't feel as sorry for myself as that sounds, honestly." And he walked his black horse out the barn door.

"Where are you off to now?" I asked. "I thought we'd ride into Sisseton and get a room at a hotel for a change. What do you think of that, son?" Jonathan's eyes sparkled as he nodded in agreement. "Soak in a good hot soapy tub, get a shave and some real haircuts at a barber, they do have a barber don't they? They must have, after all, the town is four years old all ready, they say." Looking down at me, he said seriously, "Maggie, I'm going to be stopping back in a day or two. Could we talk again? Don't go doing anything rash in the meantime. An old lady of thirty-eight shouldn't make sudden decisions you know!" And with a smile and a wink he was gone in a cloud of dust with Jonathan beside him.

I went back to digging the garden in the cool of the evening, but my heart wasn't in it. I finally put the shovel and hoe away and sat on my step thinking about the last two hours. "Now what did that all mean?" I asked myself. "What right does he have, barging into my life again and acting like he has something to say about what I do?" I could have kicked myself for the thoughtless speech about wishing Jonathan had been my son. "When will you ever learn to hold your tongue Margaret?" What a shocking statement to make to a man. At first it had seemed perfectly natural to tell Charlie what I was thinking just as I always had, but the more I thought of it the worse I felt. Burying my hot face in my hands I wondered what Marcus would say if he had heard it. He would be appalled, and would take back his proposal in a minute.

As the sun was slipping behind the hills, I remembered there were chores to do before going in for supper. My setting hens needed to be fed and watered, and a few pieces of washing were still hanging on the line behind the house. They would be getting damp again in the evening dew if I didn't take them in right away. So putting all the disturbing thoughts away, I hurried to finish up outside before it was completely dark.

True to his word Charlie and Jonathan were back in two days. They were both sporting new clothes and haircuts. Jonathan's hair had only been trimmed and left collar length as many Indian boys wore it. I was out in my garden that finally had gotten worked enough to plant a few seeds. Waiting while I finished the row of peas, Charlie told me what they planned to do that day. "I want to take Jonathan to the school and see what it's like. Will anyone be there do you think?" I was sure the cleaning people were working while the pupils were away so I told him that the doors should be open, and no one would mind if they went in and looked around. "Come with us Maggie, would you please?" He asked. "You can tell us all about it...come on...I'll saddle Buttercup for you." But I answered, "Instead, why don't you hitch her to the buggy while I change my dress. We can all fit in the buggy and you can leave your horses here...or you could ride your pony beside us Jonathan. I don't ride much anymore, I've gotten so used to driving the buggy everywhere."

We started for the school with Charlie at the reins and Jonathan riding his pony. It was odd, but I had forgotten my embarrassment of the evening of their arrival and was only enjoying the company of Charlie and his son. We met two other buggies on our way, people of the township, and as we acknowledged each other with a nod and a wave I noticed their curious stares at my companions. "Ah well," I thought, "This will start tongues wagging I suppose."

While we drove, I told them how the school was operated. Before the children had left for their vacation, they had helped to plant a large vegetable garden, which was tended and harvested and used for food in the fall and winter months. Meat was also butchered and preserved. The parents would bring deer and other game to the school, which also helped to feed the children. Of course the federal government funded the school itself. There was 640 acres of land along with the school building site. Boys were taught useful trades and the girls domestic science. As one of the older teachers had put it when I was starting, "We don't want to turn them into white people, but if we can teach the children how to live in this new world that has been forced upon them, we will be accomplishing something." Nearly all the families had been converted to Christianity, but the old superstitions might take generations to change.

We walked all around the schoolrooms, and took a look at the dormitories. When we spoke about the children who lived at the school, Jonathan looked a question at his father, but said nothing. Charlie just laid a hand on his shoulder, and said in answer to the unspoken query, "We'll see, son, we'll see." He glanced across at me then, and I could see the sadness in his eyes, and understood how much he would hate to leave Jonathan behind when he moved on.

We were quiet on the ride back, Charlie seemed to be deep in thought, and I didn't want to interrupt. As he unhitched Buttercup and put her in the barn, I asked if they would stay for dinner, but Charlie said that he had some things to see to in town, and could we make it another time?

Marcus called on me later in the week and asked if we could go for a drive, so I put on my bonnet and he helped me into his buggy. He took the road south through the coulee where the trail wound around till we were to the crest of the hills. I loved the view from up here; the whole valley lay spread out before us. Over to the north Lake Traverse was just visible, and on a very clear day Big Stone might be seen to the east if we looked closely. It didn't seem Marcus was interested in the view however. "Oh mercy," I sighed to myself, "Another man with something on his mind that he can't spit out. Why can't they just say what's bothering them right off and get it over with?"

After clearing his throat several times and shifting around uneasily, Marcus finally said what was troubling him. "I have been hearing about a gentleman and young Indian boy who have been spending time at your place, and that you were seen out riding with them just a day or two ago. What do you have to say about it Margaret?" I stared at him first in surprise and then in anger...but in the end my unfortunate habit of giggling at the wrong time took over, as I saw his pompously injured look. I just couldn't help myself, and as the laughter bubbled out, he looked more outraged than ever. "Well! I'm sorry you find it so amusing, but I really think you owe me an explanation. After all, we are practically promised to each other, and it certainly doesn't bode well for the future if you do things behind my back."

This had the desired effect of stopping my laughing abruptly. Instead the anger began to simmer and threaten to boil over. But this time I managed to keep it under control as I answered evenly, "But you must remember Marcus, that I have NOT given you an answer yet, and in that case I don't believe you have the right to tell me with whom to spend my time." To this he replied, "I didn't like to remind you of it Margaret, but given the matter of your divorce, you should really behave most circumspectly, or gossip will always follow you."

I bit my lip in fury, but held my tongue until I could say almost civilly, "I would appreciate you driving me home now Marcus. I believe I have had quite enough for one day. I just remembered something that must be done yet this afternoon." I turned away from him and didn't speak again until we pulled up at my door, where I didn't wait for him to help me get out. I gathered my skirts in one hand, not caring how much leg I exposed, and clambered out ungracefully. "Now wait a minute Margaret," he sputtered as I turned to go in. "You can't just leave it like this. You know I am right...I have the welfare of my children to think of, you know." "Yes, Marcus," I managed to say quietly, "I know you do, and perhaps we had better drop the idea of marriage right now as you seem to be regretting your proposal." With that, I went in the house and closed the door, throwing my bonnet on the table in disgust. "Well!" I said out loud to the stove and cupboard, "That's it! I always knew he was a stuffed shirt, but never realized he was a pompous goat on top of it." But then I noticed something strange...my heart suddenly felt lighter than it had in a long time. It was like a weight had been lifted and I was free again, free to go on with my life whichever direction it went from here. Circumspectly? I hadn't heard that word used in years...and began to laugh again as I went about my work.

We had some good showers of rain the next few days and my garden was beginning to peek through enough so I could see the rows. The beans were popping out one after the other, and the lettuce was about an inch high. It would be good to have fresh green things to eat again after a winter of dried foods. I put on heavy gloves, and with a shears in my pocket went out to pick wild roses from the roadside. They were thorny little rascals, but so beautiful that I couldn't resist cutting at least one bouquet every spring.

While I was walking home, my arms laden with blossoms, I saw two riders coming from the north toward me. When they got closer I could see it was Charlie and Jonathan and smiled to myself. As they stopped beside me, Charlie leaned over and said softly, "Isn't that a pretty sight Jonathan?" But he was looking at me, not at the roses, and Jonathan said slyly, "Yes Father, I think wild roses are very beautiful too," as he gave me a grin behind Charlie's back. "I would offer you a lift Maggie, but with those thorns I don't think we should risk putting you on Dancer," and he got down and walked beside me, leading his horse by the reins.

When we got home they both came in with me while I found a vase for the roses and set them on the table. Charlie seemed different somehow and I wondered what it was, but before I could ask, he said to me, "You seem different somehow Maggie...why?" At that I had to laugh out loud, as I explained that I was about to ask him the same question. "I have a good reason to look a bit happier, would you believe that I have found a job, and have decided to stay? Neither Jonathan nor I liked the idea of us being separated for months at a time while he was in school. This way, he can stay at the dormitory during the week, and I can bring him home with me for the weekends." Now why did that make me feel so good I wondered? I was happy for them, but it was no reason for my heart to beat faster was it?

"What kind of a job is it?" I asked to take my mind off the question in my head. "It's just a start, but I'll be working for the newspaper in Sisseton. Gathering articles and editing and such. Guess I've had enough experience at it if I haven't forgotten it all." I looked up at him and said quietly, "I'm glad you decided to stay, Charlie, it will be much better for Jonathan. An eight year old shouldn't be separated from his parents unless absolutely necessary. We see the loneliness of children all the time...the ones whose parents live far from here and can only come on special occasions. It's a hard adjustment to make, and some never do. We have had children run away, and find their way back home on foot."

While I stirred up the fire and set a pot of water on for coffee, I asked where they would be living. Charlie said that for the time being he was renting two rooms over the newspaper shop until he could find something better. "I want to build us a house out in the country eventually, where we can have a few horses and a cow. I'm no farmer as you know Maggie, but still would like to be where we can call a few acres our own."

"Enough about us, now tell me what put that carefree look back on your face, the one I hadn't seen since I've been here? Does it have something to do with the steady, sober, upstanding widower? You know the one I mean...The pillar of the community, and all that?" He had that wary look back in his eye again, as he watched me set out the cups and saucers and put cookies on a plate. I didn't answer until I had poured a glass of milk for Jonathan, and then I told him, "That's over and done with. He let me see what a straightlaced person he really is, and that you were right, he had my divorce in the back of his mind all the time. He probably would have always held it over my head. People had noticed you being here and us out riding together and reported back to him. But that's all right. I'm glad to have it settled, and I feel fine...It wouldn't have worked anyway. I could never put up with a man who thought he should have everything to say about what I do." At this, Charlie gave a hoot of laughter, and jumped up taking me with him and nearly upsetting the table. He spun us around a couple of times before sitting down with me on his lap. "Now Maggie...maybe we can get to my other reason for coming back to Dakota." "And what might that be Charlie?" I asked with pretended shyness, as I tried to catch my breath. Jonathan was watching our carrying on with interest, but seemed more concerned with keeping the milk and cookies from spilling, as I put my arms around his father's neck. I asked again, looking into those beautiful blue eyes..."What was the reason Charlie?" "Do you suppose," he began hesitantly, "That a washed up has been and an over the hill thirty-eight year old could find happiness together this late in life?" "Do you mean this widower is looking for a mother for his child and a housekeeper, and is willing to overlook the scandal of my divorce?" I couldn't help teasing him as I tightened my arms around him and buried my face in his shoulder. "Oh Maggie, will you just hush your mouth for once in your life and give me a kiss?"

June 30, 1896...Sofie beamed happily as she helped button the cuffs of my dress, then turned me toward the mirror so we could see how I looked. "There now!" She nodded her approval, "If you don't look jes' fine, not a day over thirty, I'd say, if I dint know better." "Oh Sofie!" I protested, "That's not true, and you know it, but thanks anyway for saying it." I knew the years had not been altogether kind to me, but somehow it didn't matter so much anymore. "Come on now, we got to hurry up, they'll be waitin' on us in there," and she hustled me along, grabbing my bouquet of wild flowers from the dresser on our way. "Wait! I jes thought o' somethin'!" She whispered worriedly, "Do you 'spose Charlie remembered to get a ring on sech short notice?" "Yes Sofie, we have a ring...it's silver and turquoise with Indian carving all around, made just for me, remember?" "I remember," she nodded, as we walked into the parlor where Charlie stood with Luke and Jonathan. The minister opened his Bible and began..."Dearly Beloved...

## CHAPTER 18

**Summer, 1997**

As the rented car turned onto the busy street that led to the interstate, she cranked down the window, then cranked up the volume of the country music station that the last person to drive the car had listened to. Tapping her fingers on the steering wheel absently to the beat of the music she watched for the red white and blue sign that would say I-29 North. Spotting it, she quickly changed lanes to turn left, behind a semi truck loaded with farm machinery. Once off the ramp and on the smooth four-lane highway she stepped on the gas and passed the truck, giving the driver a friendly wave as he was left behind. Setting the cruise control at 75 she settled back to enjoy the drive on this wonderfully empty road that seemed to stretch on forever. "Heaven," she sighed happily, "Absolute heaven, where is all the traffic? I love it!" Realizing she was talking to herself, she laughed out loud and turned the radio up some more as an Alan Jackson hit from two years ago began to play.

With the wind blowing her hair in all directions, she watched the green fields flying past her window...rows of corn, wheat blowing like waves on water, and fragrant windrows of hay being rolled into large bales. Black cattle were grazing a pasture in grass up to their knees. Everything looked lush and peaceful to this city girl, accustomed as she was to traffic and crowds of people everywhere on the streets. Ponds of water reflected the blue of the skies and made a change from the many shades of green that are the color of northeastern South Dakota in June. A large billboard advertising a casino a few miles to the west didn't interest her, and she sped past the exit and continued her way north.

Abigail Preston was a woman on a mission, and would not be sidetracked, by enticing signs to right or left, until she had found what she was looking for. Her chin had a stubborn firmness about it that told of a person with a mind of her own. She was on her way to Peever, fifty some miles up the interstate, and her mission was to find out more about her great-great-great grandparents. Her hometown was Philadelphia, the City of Brotherly Love. "What a joke," she thought bitterly, as she allowed her thoughts to dwell for a minute on the spoiled discontented relatives and friends that she had left behind. Only for a minute though, then she went back to watching the passing scenery, as the landscape seemed to be changing from farmland into hilly grassland with many more patches of blue water. Herds of various colored cattle dotted the pastures, where sturdy barbed wire fences kept them from wandering onto the highway. Scattered piles of stones told of the effort of ranchers to clear some of the rocky land.

A green sign announcing she had reached the Roberts County line brought a smile to her lips, as she knew she had nearly reached her destination. A few minutes later she passed an exit to a rest stop and another sign said "Sisseton, 17 miles." That would be her goal tonight, as she knew there were no motels in the little town of Peever, and would need a place to live during her stay.

Now she was at the crest of the hills with a beautiful view of the valley laid out below. The road curved gently down as her ears plugged unpleasantly, and she swallowed hard to clear them. A few miles further on she spotted the Peever exit with its sign proclaiming there was food and fuel to be had there. Craning her neck to the east she could see the water tower and a line of trees showing the town was very near the highway. "I'll be back in the morning, so stay right there till I get back," she chuckled to the little town in the valley, and moved to the left lane to allow a dusty red pickup room to get onto the highway from the ramp.

Exiting at the Sisseton and Browns Valley turnoff, Abigail was soon at a motel on the outskirts of town where she was able to rent a room for a week, paying in advance with her overworked Visa card. "Oh well," she shrugged to herself, "It's a once in a lifetime thing, and soon as I'm working again it'll get paid off easily enough." Locking her door and tossing clothes on the bed she stepped into the shower to wash away all traces of the long day's travels.

With the lovely warm water streaming over her she was remembering her great-great-great grandmother's account of the train trip to Dakota Territory in 1883..."I had never felt so grubby and disheveled in my life," when she arrived at the town where she would began teaching school in a few weeks. "Oh Grandma," Abigail thought to herself, "I wish I had known you. You seem so much like me, I bet we would have understood each other."

Abigail didn't fully realize it, but she was very like her ancestor Margaret Sinclair Preston who had braved the wrath of her father to come west and start a life of her own. She had the same straight nose and deep set eyes, the same independent nature that demanded something different in life than her parents had. She had annoyed both of them by not conforming to their idea of what she should do when finished with the four years at Penn State. Instead of going on to graduate school, she had taken a job in downtown Philadelphia working for a second rate newspaper.

Digging through her luggage, she chose a pair of slightly wrinkled cotton shorts and a green Philadelphia Eagles tee shirt, then sat down at the mirror to brush the tangles out of the dark brown hair that hung wetly around her face. Her tanned face needed no makeup, but she dabbed on a bit of lipstick, and got up to put away the rest of her clothes in the closet and dresser drawers. Her growling stomach let her know it was time for supper, so she slung her small purse over her shoulder, and grabbed the keys. Turning back she took a small book out of her tote bag to read while she ate.

A tiny restaurant was on the south side of the two lane highway not far from the motel, and seeing the menu posted outside advertising a small steak for 5.99, she quickly turned in and parked. "Wow," she muttered to herself, "That's cheap. It's worth a try, the shape my finances are in." The window boxes on the north were over flowing with beautiful flowers and Abigail stopped briefly to admire them before going in. The new little building was lovely and cool, and quite empty as it was late for the supper crowd on a weeknight in farm country. She laid her things on a table by the window overlooking the highway after ordering steak at the counter.

Choosing her salads and settling down to eat she took the book out of her purse and thumbed through it until she found what she was looking for. The light from the window was needed to make out the faded writing Margaret Preston had penned so many years ago. "Today Charlie asked if I would be willing to move to the new town that has been started just a few miles east of here. There would be an opportunity for him to write his own newspaper again, and he would like that. I can't fault him for wanting to have a business, but I do rather dread to think of leaving our comfortable home here in the foothills. They say the land Peever is built on is rather swampy as it is on the edge of a large slough. But I will do as he wishes as I'm sure it will be for the best in the long run."

Finishing her salad Abigail pushed her plate aside and turned the pages back toward the front of the diary to September of 1898. She loved this part of her grandmother's journal..."Soon I must tell Charlie my news about the baby. I'm afraid he will think we are too old, but not much we can do about it now. I'm thrilled to death to be having a child at last. Jonathan will have a little brother or sister before spring comes. I hope they will both be glad. Charlie is all involved in another courthouse battle. This time it is between Sisseton and Wilmot. I'm just mean enough to be happy that Wilmot might lose it after the tricks they pulled to get it away from us at Travare. They will get no sympathy from us. It would be to our advantage to have the county seat in Sisseton anyway. It has always been a thorn in my side to have to go to Wilmot on county business and see our courthouse on their main street."

As Abigail stared out the window at the setting sun over the Coteau Hills, she could imagine her grandparents looking at the same hills and almost heard their voices.

"Maggie! Maggie!" Charlie called as he bounded up the back steps waving a newspaper like a flag and flinging open the kitchen door. I knew he had some great news as I had heard Dancer galloping up the drive and had gotten up to look out the window. I watched as he leaped off and hastily tied his stallion to a post on the yard fence. "Look! There's going to be another election after all, and this time we are going to win. I'm not a betting man, but I would bet my last shirt that people will be fired up enough this time to get out and vote." Last time the vote had been light because of the lack of interest or knowledge of what was going on and Wilmot had gained the majority.

"That's wonderful dear, I'm glad it might finally be settled. Then I hope that's the last we have to hear of quarreling over the county seat in Roberts County...ever." I read the article on the front page of the paper with interest, before asking Charlie if he would be ready for supper soon. "Got to take care of Dancer and check on things outside first. Where's Jon? I didn't see him around anywhere as I rode up." "He's over at the church helping the Reverend with some fall clean up on the grounds. He should be back soon." I answered. At this Charlie scowled a little as he grumbled, "I swear, that boy spends more time at the church than he does at home. I guess I should get some more livestock so that he has enough chores to do around here to keep him busy." I raised my brows a bit at his remark, and couldn't help retorting that there were worse things Jon could be doing than spending time with the preacher. "I know, I know," Charlie replied sheepishly. "I guess I'm not really complaining but...it just seems like he has more to say to Reverend Michaels than he does to me lately." "Well my dear, you have been busy and distracted of late," I reminded him, "And the Reverend has always had an interest in Jon so it isn't surprising he would turn to him as a friend. I'm sure it doesn't mean that he doesn't want to be with you. He has enjoyed hearing the stories of the mission field out west of the river where the pastor was before coming here." At this Charlie smiled his old happy grin and leaned over to give me a kiss as he said, "Oh Maggie, you are the sensible one, you can always set me straight if I only listen. I'll be in shortly to eat if you have it ready, then I'll do the milking later. It's a little too early yet for that."

While I stirred up the fire to start supper, I thought back to the time before we were married two years ago. After we had set the day of our wedding Charlie and I had a long talk about his reasons for coming back to Dakota with his son. "It was more than just wanting Jon to have schooling Maggie," he told me. "You know how I was when I left...so full of myself...but I had no faith to carry me through the disappointments of losing our town and my dreams. Even if it meant losing you, I couldn't stay and face it. Then when Jon's mother and everyone died I realized at last that I needed God to help me and prayed for strength and faith to take care of my boy. There were no missions yet in that remote part of Montana, and Pah-HA-ton-kah wah'-CHA and her people were of the old religion. I knew in my heart it wasn't right, and when Jonathan got older what I wanted for him was to know the Christian teachings and Jesus as his Savior." My eyes filled with tears as I heard this confession of faith from the strong self reliant man that I had loved for so long, and it brought a lump to my throat as I thought of it yet.

It was such a blessing to hear the children and Jonathan with them singing on Sunday morning in Dakotah..."Wah-NE-ke-yah Chon-t'kin-yah me-YEH, deh me-YEH s'dod-YAH"...(Jesus loves me, this I know). Charlie's eyes would shine with love and pride watching his son and I knew he had done the right thing.

As the biscuits were baking Jonathan came riding in on his pony and I was glad to see him talking to Charlie out by the barn. He had become such a good-looking ten-year-old and I felt as much pride in him as if he were my own flesh and blood. After one year at the government school his knowledge of reading and writing were far advanced of some of the other children because Charlie had been teaching him the letters long before they had come back. After that we transferred him to the Goodwill Mission school, because he knew English as well as anyone. Now with the fall term his class would be studying division of numbers and other harder arithmetic problems along with sentence structure. My teaching days were over and I kept busy enough with home, family and church work. With the baby coming I would have plenty to occupy my time.

While Charlie and Jon were washing up at the basin in the corner I got supper on the table. Warmed up potatoes with fried onions, scrambled eggs, sliced tomatoes and the hot biscuits made a hearty meal for a growing boy and busy man. As for me, the sight of the eggs in the blue pottery bowl turned my stomach and I had to run for the door where I leaned on the gate in the agony of dry heaves. With tears streaming down my face I turned to see Charlie behind me shaking his head with a wry smile. Putting his arms around me gently he whispered softly, "All right Maggie, are you ready to tell me now, or are you going to keep it a secret until the day our child is born?" "H-how did you guess?" I quavered miserably, leaning on his chest while the nausea began to subside. "Do you think me a complete fool, or just a blind man who can't notice anything?" He laughed, as he picked me up in his arms and carried me back to the kitchen steps. "You weigh next to nothing anymore," he scolded. "I know you haven't been eating much, but I didn't realize how much you have lost. You better be able to keep food down pretty soon or you'll be down to skin and bones." I looked up to see Jon watching through the screen door and his face was white with fright. "Are you all right Mother?" He asked shakily. "Oh Jonny, don't look so scared! I'm fine. Just a little upset stomach, nothing to worry about. Come on now and eat your supper before it gets cold." I managed to sit at my place and eat half a biscuit and two slices of tomatoes while Charlie smiled at me encouragingly.

"What would you think son, of having a brother or sister?" He asked as Jon took a second helping of fried potatoes. "Why?" the boy asked curiously looking from Charlie to me, and then back to his father again. "Well," Charlie answered him..."Along about next March your mother is going to have a baby, so you and I are going to have to take good care of her and see that she doesn't work too hard, understand?" Jon's eyes opened wide in surprise, and he exclaimed, "I think that's a wonderful idea! I can't wait to tell my friends...they all have brothers and sisters, now I will too!" His father laughed, "Whoa there a minute, I don't think your mother wants you spreading the news around the township just yet, all right? We better just keep it a secret between the three of us for the time being." Jon grinned and replied, "I can keep a secret as good as anyone, you'll see. And from now on I'll bring the water and wood up for you every day." "Thank you Jon, I will appreciate that," I sighed gratefully, as I breathed a prayer of thanks that my men were happy about the news.

# CHAPTER 19

"Here's your supper miss," the waitress said as she set the steaming plate of hash browns and medium rare steak in front of Abigail. Startled back to the present, she shook her head slightly to clear it and smiled her thanks to the young girl who served her. She was a pretty black haired teenager with the Native American heritage obvious in her high cheekbones and dark eyes.

The long Dakota twilight was spreading over the countryside and Abigail could see the evening star in the western sky, as she chewed her steak hungrily. "M-mmm this is great," she murmured while the waitress filled her water glass again. "You staying at the motel?" The waitress asked curiously. "You're from away aren't ya? I can tell by the way you talk." "Why, do I sound different?" Abigail asked in surprise. "Oh yeah," the girl replied, "I had some cousins last year from the east come and visit, and you sound sorta like they did. I noticed your license plate is South Dakota though so I could be wrong, I guess." She turned away, picking up Abigail's salad plate as she started toward the kitchen. "You're pretty observant, I'd say," Abigail chuckled, "And you are right. I'm from Philadelphia, and the car is rented from Watertown." The waitress tossed her ponytail back and gave her a sunny smile as she disappeared through the kitchen door.

Her meal over, Abigail left the restaurant wondering how to spend the evening. "Guess I'll go check out the town before turning in," she thought. Town wasn't far away; just a short drive west brought her to Main Street. Driving slowly through, she saw there was not much going on this evening. A grocery store parking lot had several cars and pickup trucks with teenagers standing around talking and killing time as teenagers do. On the hill to the east she saw the domed building that must be the courthouse for the county, so she took a right turn and drove up the hill to see it better. An attractive building and she knew what year it had been built thanks to her grandmother's journal. "I probably know more about the early history of this building and Roberts County than any of these kids who live here," Abigail thought as she drove through the residential streets and back to the highway.

# CHAPTER 20

**Fall, 1898** — As we lay in bed later that night, I turned to Charlie and asked, "Honestly now, don't you think we are too old to be having a baby? We're going to be old and gray, well...grayer," I added with a giggle making a concession to the silver hairs that were becoming more evident for both of us, "By the time she is twenty-one." "It's SHE all ready is it?" He teased as he pulled my braid playfully. "That's fine with me...I'd like to have a daughter. Oh I can see her now, headstrong and outspoken and bound and determined to have her own way!" "Are you implying that she would be inheriting those traits from her mother?" I teased, curling up beside him, feeling more content than I had in weeks. "Wouldn't have you any other way, wife o' mine," he replied softly. "I don't know what I did to deserve being this happy. It scares me sometimes...like it's too good to last." "Well now...you just put those thoughts out of your head. Things will be just fine, you'll see." I predicted cheerfully, as my eyes began to be heavy with sleep.

And so the autumn days slipped by, all blue and gold, with the cooling breezes that were a welcome change from the hot summer of the prairie. The sumac was red on the hillsides and the wild grapes and other berries had been picked for jelly. People were planning for the worst again, as anyone with an ounce of sense did not go into a South Dakota winter without preparation. School had begun at the mission and Jon was enjoying the routine and being at the head of his class. Occasionally I helped him with a thorny arithmetic problem, or complicated sentence that had to be diagrammed. He loved his Sunday School lessons, and they were first on his list of things to do at the beginning of the week. Reverend Michaels was still one of his heroes and Jon was forever repeating the stories he had told him of his years in the Wild West among the Indian tribes.

Thankfully I had gotten over the nausea that had plagued me at the outset of my pregnancy, and was beginning to put on weight again. The baby was moving and kicking with a healthy abandon, especially when I was lying down trying to rest. "Would you feel that!" Charlie would exclaim as he laid his hand on my stomach to check on his daughter. "If she isn't a lively one! I can see it might be a full time job keeping track of that girl once she gets to walking." So I would sit in my rocker sewing tiny clothes in the evenings while Charlie sat at the table writing new articles for the paper. He would look over his glasses from time to time and give me a contented smile, and I would realize once more how lucky we had been to find each other again.

November came and time for the election. We were elated that Sisseton had gained enough votes in the county seat issue to give them the majority. Although, as in the past, this was not the end of it. Wilmot was going to make an appeal in the courts. But with some negotiating, it was agreed that Sisseton would pay $1000.00 in reimbursement to Wilmot for expenses, and in that way prevent a more costly battle.

It turned out to be a ticklish ordeal even so as some of the men became uneasy and distrustful, and it was arranged secretly to go on the night of November 17th to remove the records at once instead of waiting until the next day as was first decided. Someone had heard of a plan of some of the Wilmot men to go to Milbank to ask the judge for a temporary injunction restraining the county officers from moving, until the court had passed upon the legality of the election. And so teams were hitched up and some of the men made the trip to Wilmot in the dark of night. Charlie naturally had to be in the thick of things despite my misgivings. I had not forgotten what had happened to him the night the records were stolen from Travare. Stealthily, they managed to load everything in the wagons and got out of town without being apprehended. It took the rest of the night to get back to Sisseton, and they came into town where the church bells were ringing in celebration while the sun was just coming up.

Jonathan and I of course heard all this when Charlie finally got home. We had spent a restless night wondering what was happening, and when after dawn we heard Dancer galloping up the driveway we both breathed a sigh of relief. Jon ran out to meet him and I followed, but more slowly, as I didn't want to tumble down the porch steps in my condition. His big smile told us what we needed to know, and we all sat down in the kitchen while he told us the whole story. "And of course the town constable had to notice us, and ask what we were doing, but we managed to convince him to keep his mouth shut. Now, my dear...could I please have some breakfast? I'm starving!" And he kissed the top of my head as he went to put more wood on the fire.

Winter was settling in to stay now, but we were warm and cozy in our snug house. I had a good supply of dried vegetables and fruits put away, and Charlie hadn't forgotten his skills as a hunter and trapper so we had our meat and some warm furs. Jon had learned from his father and could snare a rabbit or shoot a prairie chicken as well as any man.

One Sunday when we had been enjoying a stretch of warm weather, we were surprised and happy to see Sofie and Luke in our congregation. They didn't often get over this way, as it was about eight miles to their place. I gave Sofie a warm hug as we sat beside them, and she whispered, "We took a chance that you'd be home today. I brung some stuff for dinner, thought we could catch up on everthing that's been happning before the weather gets too bad." "Oh Sofie, that was a wonderful idea, it seems like such a long time since we have seen you." Glad that I had baked a couple of pies on Saturday and put a venison roast in the oven before we left, I knew that there would be plenty to eat. As Reverend Michaels came in we all stood for the opening hymn, and it was good to have our friends beside us in church again as in the old days.

As Sofie and I got the meal on the table we talked constantly...about the new baby, how Ben was doing with his family, and their harvest, which had been good this year. "Besides we had ten head o'steers to sell this year! Isn't that somethin'?" She told me happily. "Now we can add a bit o' room to the house fin'lly. I had got used to that big kitchen at the hotel, and it jest seems like I got no room to turn 'round in. But we dint get it started this fall, so will have to wait til spring I guess, but that's alright. I'll have it to look forward to longer."

After the dishes were done, we all gathered around the piano while I played and everyone sang. We sang our favorites from the hymnbook, and some old songs that we remembered as children, and a few of the newer ones. All in all it was a wonderful day. After I had made another pot of coffee and everyone had one more piece of pie, Luke hitched up the sleigh to go home. "Margret," Sofie remarked, "You take care o' yourself the rest o' the winter. I want that Godchild o' ours to be born in good shape!" She looked at me seriously, and I knew that she was concerned, but I tried to keep a light tone, as I answered, "We are going to be fine Sofie, don't you worry, Charlie and Jon take good care of me. Anyway, I hope we see you before then...if the weather is fit, maybe we can get together at Christmas?" I looked at Charlie hopefully, and he put his hand on my shoulder as he shook his head, "I am not taking you out for an eight mile sleigh ride when you are seven months along in the dead of winter. But if you two are up to it, come over on the 24th and spend the night. We can go to Christmas Eve service and have some time together. Could you leave your livestock for a couple of days?" He asked Luke. "I can probably get the neighbor to come and look after things for once. The cows have to be milked, otherwise we could leave the other stock with enough feed and water. But we will see how it goes and let you know. Sofie can drop you a letter when the time gets closer." And with that he clucked to his horses and they glided away in the pale afternoon sun. Sofie waved until they were out of sight, and with a sigh I returned to the warmth of the kitchen.

I had begun clearing away the pie plates feeling downhearted at saying goodbye to our two best friends, when Charlie came up behind me and put both arms around me tightly. Rocking me gently against him, he whispered, "Don't be sad baby, you still got me," and he chuckled softly in my ear. Turning around I laid my face against his chest as I mumbled into his shirt, "I'm not sad really, it's just that I miss seeing Sofie like we used to. I never did make a friend that meant as much to me as she does." "I know, I know," he answered. "Maybe someday we can live closer, who can tell?"

## CHAPTER 21

The alarm on her watch beeped insistently until Abigail at last opened her eyes and with one bewildered look around remembered where she was. "This is the day! I'm going to Peever at last, at last!" she sang happily while turning on the shower. She didn't think the name Peever odd, like many people who hear it for the first time because she all ready knew it was named after it's founder Thomas H. Peever.

After dressing in jeans and pullover shirt, she gathered all her notes, paper, diaries, and one lone postcard with a picture of main street from about 1910. The photo showed a full row of buildings along the east side of the street, a bustling little town after the turn of the century. One building beside the store on the corner looked as if it might have been a hotel and she wondered if that was the one...?

The clouds hung over the hills in the west, looking as if a shower of rain might be coming before long, and the air smelled damp and was mixed with the aroma of new mown hay from the fields along the road. Abigail turned back onto the interstate that she had driven last night, thinking that when she returned later today she would take another road to see more of the countryside. But she was in a hurry this morning and wanted to get on with her quest. She had a styrofoam cup of coffee in the cup holder, and occasionally would take a gulp. "Ugh," she muttered to herself, "Weak again! Don't they know how to make coffee in South Dakota?" She was accustomed to the strong East Coast coffee that she would lace with cream and sugar, but drank it anyway, promising herself she would make her own if able to bring a coffee maker into the motel room.

The smooth road brought her to the Peever exit in a very few minutes, and she looked again with interest at the signs that pointed west. Tribal Headquarters...and Community College, one read. "H'mmm, that would be the Agency, I bet...where grandma and grandpa and Jonathan lived for awhile. The school would have been there that grandma taught, too. I must go out there later today. There are so many things to look for...hope someone can help me..." All these thoughts were running through Abigail's head as she stopped at the end of the ramp and signaled to turn left.

A busy little truck stop was immediately off the exit, and she made a note of it as a place to stop for gas that would also take her cash card. She almost held her breath on the short drive to the outskirts of town, wondering what she would see. When she crossed the tracks and passed an implement shop she realized she was on the eastern edge and put on her brakes in surprise. "Mercy!" she exclaimed aloud, "I nearly missed it. Got to turn around and go back and find Main Street."

Driving slower this time she crossed the tracks once more, this time seeing the turn to what looked as if might be a business district. The sun came out brightly just then and as Abigail drove the length of Main Street of Peever she looked right and left in total shock. Finally she pulled into the last business on the street which was a small service station, and shut the car off. Getting out with legs that felt like pudding was a bit of a problem, but finally she got her wits back enough to look around some more. "Where did everything go? There's nothing left of Main Street. Where are all the buildings? How will I ever find out anything if there are no buildings left?" she thought as she hung on to the door of the car.

A tall thin man wiping his hands on a grease rag came out and looked at her curiously, then asked if he could help her with something. He secretly suspected that this young lady had too much to drink from the dazed look on her face. "Oh no thank you," Abigail replied absently, "I was just looking around." Then she blurted, "What happened to everything?" He looked at her like she was something dropped from outer space and asked cautiously. "What do you mean...what happened to everything? What everything?" She flapped her hands at the bare street and replied weakly, "All the businesses...the banks...the stores. The newspaper office...Where IS the newspaper office?" "Oh my! We haven't had a newspaper for so many years that I'm sure I have no idea where it would have been," he laughed. "Are you sure you are all right?" he asked carefully, thinking this was the strangest person he had encountered for many a day. "Fires...Several fires." He finally thought to answer Abigail's agonized questions. "The one in 1915 kinda cleaned out a lot of the original buildings along the west side here. Then they rebuilt. There were more fires throughout the years until most the oldest ones were gone. Except for our building, the café on the corner down there and a couple of others."

Abigail was beginning to feel like herself again, and decided that this friendly man might be able to help her. She realized that he had been looking at her strangely, so she said with an embarrassed chuckle,

"I guess you thought I was totally nuts the way I sounded, but it is so disappointing. I came all this way to find out about my grandparents, and now I wonder if there is any sign of them left anywhere. Besides their graves...which might be hard to find, too. Maybe not even marked..." She rambled on as he continued to watch her with interest. "Well now, someone will be able to tell you about that at least. I was just going down for coffee, why don't you come along and talk to someone at the café. We can always call for the cemetery records if no one knows exactly where it is. Besides our cemetery isn't that big but what you could probably find them if the graves are marked at all." So calling for his wife to come along he said, "Just leave your car parked here and we'll walk down the block and have coffee and see if Connie has time to talk." Locking the car after she took out her things, Abigail introduced herself. They told her they were the Webers...Bill and Jeanne, and had been in business for forty years, give or take a few, and ready to retire soon. "Trouble is, no one wants to take over a place like this anymore, so it will probably just close once we quit. Same problem with the café...Folks don't want to put in the kind of hours it takes to keep places like this going day in and day out."

Entering the old building on the corner, Abigail blinked her eyes to accustom them to the dim interior after the brightness of the street, and followed Jeanne to a booth while Bill poured coffee for all of them. "Hey Connie," he called to the older woman who came out of the kitchen to check who had come in, "Come see who we brought you...all the way from Philadelphia. She came to pick your brains about the early days of Peever that you are so crazy about. This here is Connie Martin...Abigail Preston."...He made the introduction while investigating the contents of the jars on the counter. "You two want a doughnut with your coffee? I'll buy, I'm feeling generous today so better take me up on it!" And he looked over at Jeanne and Abigail with a twinkle in his eye. "None for me, but thanks," Abigail answered, feeling too nervous to eat anything. Instead she sipped cautiously at the coffee, finding it too weak for her taste again, but glad for the warmth in her stomach.

Sliding over to make room for Connie Martin to sit down, Jeanne remarked, "You look beat. Busy morning?" To which Connie replied with a grimace while trying unsuccessfully to tuck straggling locks of hair under her head band, "Not really, just a lot of baking to catch up on but its almost done, so I'll be glad to sit a few minutes. Here's my cup Bill, fill it for me before you sit down will you please?" And she held out a big ceramic mug with "The Boss" painted in red letters.

Sipping her coffee, she looked Abigail over closely and murmured. "Preston, you said? Well, there was a Preston who was the first editor of the *Peever Weekly*. Let me think now...what did I do with that old box of stuff with the pictures and clippings? If I would ever get these things organized so we could find what we wanted, it sure would be nice." Taking a gulp of her coffee she got up and went to an old cupboard in the corner where she got on her knees to dig in the depths of a cluttered grouping of shelves. "Aha! Found it," Connie exclaimed in triumph, as she pulled herself painfully to her feet. "I'm sorry to cause you any bother." Abigail said apologetically, as she noticed the trouble she had getting up. "It's nothing," Connie replied cheerfully, "Just old age making itself felt. When I was your age I could get up and down like a spring chicken. Anyway, we might find something in here to help." And she began to rummage about in the cardboard box that was overflowing with yellowed clippings and curling photos.

Abigail's heart had given a lurch at Connie's words and she ventured hesitantly, "My grandfather's name was Charles Preston, and I think he might have been that first editor. According to grandma's diary, they moved here soon after the town was started, and the plan had been for him to start his own newspaper again. He had been an editor years before in a town nearby...did you ever hear of Travare? It's not around anymore. It didn't last long apparently." At the mention of Travare, Connie's eyes lit up and she dropped the handful of pictures as she exclaimed, "You are kidding! Travare...Oh this is wonderful! I think I read somewhere in one of the old papers about Charlie Preston, who was one of the founders of Travare in 1883. Bill don't you remember reading that when we had those Roberts County history books around here?" To which Bill replied after he had swallowed a mouthful of doughnut that he never did pay much attention to that old stuff. Shaking her head at him reprovingly Connie scolded, "How are your grandkids ever going to know about this town and county if you don't take an interest?" And she reached down to pick her pictures off the floor.

"You have a diary of your grandmother's from the 1880s?" Connie asked. "Yes, they were found in a bunch of old stuff that was being sorted through when my parents were selling the house. My mother doesn't care much about the past either, so she just handed them all over to me to keep. The first one I have is from 1883, the year Grandma Maggie came to Dakota Territory to teach school and that's how she and Grandpa Charlie met. He was the man who hired her. And the last one I could find was from 1915. There was a big fire that year.

Seems she lost interest then in writing or the diaries were destroyed. I really don't know." She finished sadly.

"Well anyway, you have a wonderful record up to then of the early years of Roberts County. Are they in good condition so you can make out the writing easily?" Connie asked, itching to get a look at them but not wanting to ask outright. "Mostly they are in very good shape, some of the ink has faded, but she had such good penmanship, being a teacher, that I can read nearly every word." She dug in her tote bag and pulled one out randomly and handed it to Connie who took it reverently in both hands and rubbed her fingers over the leather cover. "Go ahead...open it," Abigail urged, "You can look at some of the entries if you like...this one begins at January 1892 when she was divorced from her first husband. She always wrote too much to just use the few lines in a five-year diary, so she would take almost a page at a time. Some of these only have two years in them."

"Divorced?" Jeanne exclaimed "I never thought anyone got divorced back then!" "Well. Grandma Maggie did, "Abigail answered. "She married a no good salesman who ran off with her money and another woman so she eventually got divorced from him. It must have been scandalous at the time." "I'm sure it was," Connie agreed, as she turned pages, reading bits and pieces greedily as she went. Suddenly something caught her attention and she said to the others, "Listen to this...'Today we buried Chief Renville. He died a few days ago, August 26th at Sam and Phoebe's house in Browns Valley. But he was brought here for burial, and what a wonderful spot! The highest hill just a ways south of here...overlooking everything...and the view was wonderful today. We could see all the way to the lakes. The Chief would have been pleased. The wild flowers were thick on the hilltop and we picked a few and laid them on his grave after it was covered. It was quite a climb getting up there and a struggle getting down again. I had to hang onto the small trees and shrubs as I descended so as not to go head over heels." Connie looked up from her reading to explain to Abigail that Chief Gabriel Renville was Sam Brown's uncle, and one of the main historic figures of that time. Always a peaceable man, and sensible. "He was not in favor of opening the land here for settlement but the people wanted to sell so he was out voted. He died a few months after the land rush took place."

A customer came in then and Connie had to get up and wait on him and on her way back she filled everyone's coffee cup before sitting down once more. "Someone can go with you to the cemetery to help with finding their graves," she told Abigail, "So you won't have

93

to search the whole place over. I know where they are, but I have to stay here. It'll soon be lunchtime and I better get back to work...I'll call Martha, and if she isn't too busy, she'll be glad to go with you out there." "How far away is the cemetery?" Abigail asked as she finished her coffee. "Not far," Jeanne told her, "Just outside town about a mile, walking distance, actually. That's where I take my exercise some mornings." "Jeanne," Connie asked, "Will you make that call to Martha please? Look at the time, good grief, I got to get a move on. Will you be staying awhile so we can talk again?" She turned to ask Abigail while heading back to the kitchen tying on her apron as she went. "Oh yes," was the reply. "I came out here intending to stay about a week, so will be around until I find as much information as possible. Thanks so much for your time, sorry if I made you late with your work." "Oh, no problem," Connie assured her, "It wouldn't be the first time the potatoes weren't done when the first hungry man came in!"

In a few minutes the door opened and a bundle of energy in the form of a wiry little woman came bustling in. Under her arm she carried a large folder and spotting Abigail sitting alone she came over and held out her hand, "You must be the one who is looking for me, right?" She sat down across from her and smiled in a friendly way. "I'm Martha Anderson, but I guess Connie told you that, and you are one of the Prestons from the east. Jeanne filled me in on the phone. You know, it was said that Charlie Preston's younger son left after his mother's funeral and never came back to South Dakota. Seems odd doesn't it?" "Well," Abigail said slowly, as she tried to remember what she had been told, "I think once he was grown and his parents and brother were gone he went back to Philadelphia to find the other relatives and ended up staying there. I have a lot of relation in Pennsylvania because the Sinclairs are there too, from Grandma Maggie's side."

Connie stuck her head out the kitchen door as she called over the noise of her mixer mashing potatoes; "You know where the graves are don't you Mart? Those four marble stones that look almost the same over in the northeast corner." "I know, I remember them from when we put the flowers and flags out on Memorial Day. So we'll just be off to go have a look, then come back for lunch. Whatcha having today?" She remembered to ask as they were going out the door. Connie yelled back the answer and went to take the potatoes out of the mixer bowl.

"Get in and ride with me," Martha ordered in her brisk fashion as she slid behind the wheel of her minivan and fastened her seat belt, "No sense both of us driving. Once you know where it is you can go back and spend more time if you want, O.K.?" And she started her engine and backed out carefully, looking both ways and as far behind as she could. Abigail wondered about her seemingly unnecessary care as there wasn't another car in sight until Martha answered her unspoken question..."Have to watch out for the kids here. Little ones wander around Main Street like it's a playground some days. Scares the daylights out of me." "I should think it would," shuddered Abigail making a mental note to be extra careful when she got back behind the wheel.

As they got out of the van Martha pointed to the far corner, "That's them over there. You know what? There is another married couple buried right beside them, but they don't seem to be family. The stones are almost exactly the same though. Don't know if it means anything or not."

As Abigail knelt to trace the lettering on the worn marble she felt unaccustomed tears welling up in her eyes and fumbled in her pocket for a tissue. "Oh look," she whispered, as she read the other two stones..."it's Sofie and Luke." "You know who they are?" Martha asked in surprise. "They were best friends. Sofie took grandma under her wing when she first came to Dakota Territory. Luke and grandpa were in on the building of Travare. Luke and Sofie had the hotel there." She stood then and brushed off the knees of her jeans as she asked Martha, "How far away is the site of Travare, and what direction? I'd like to go there and look around." "It's not far at all," was the answer, "Only about eight miles northeast of here," she explained pointing in that direction. "But I'm sorry, there won't be anything much to see. There's a house that stands on the foundation of the old hotel, but the way I understand it was rebuilt, so it is not the original building." "I don't care, I just want to see where it was, and see the lakes grandma wrote about and Browns Valley." "Well, you can sure do that, and it's very pretty over there this time of year. The trees have grown up thick around Lake Traverse where there were none in your grandma's time. No one has quite figured out why there were trees around Big Stone but not Traverse. S'pose it had something to do with the divide being there?" She asked, not really expecting an answer. Abigail was on her knees again reading the inscriptions on the stones more carefully.

# CHAPTER 22

I woke Charlie at 3:00 AM when the pains were coming closer together and much harder. I had realized for two hours that the time had come, but did not want to wake him too early, as he would just fret and fuss. The weather was fine for March 4th and it would not take him long to go fetch the doctor from Sisseton...His eyes flew open at once as I shook his shoulder, "What...what is it Maggie! Are you all right?" "Yes, yes, I'm fine," I whispered, not wanting to wake Jon. "But I think you had better go after the doctor now, the pains are coming closer together." "Well, why didn't you wake me sooner? He could have been here by now!" He scolded. "Now you know that's not necessary, it's going to take long enough without having the poor man sitting here waiting for hours. But get up now and get started," I gasped as another pain came strongly and nearly doubled me over. He looked at me in alarm and leapt up as I fought for breath and hung onto the bedpost for support. "How can I leave you like this?" he demanded in agitation as he tried to put his trousers on back to front and yanked them off impatiently. "Charlie, Charlie, I will be fine till you get back. My goodness, this isn't your first child. Were you like this when Jon was born?" "Good grief no, I wasn't allowed anywhere near. The women of the village took care of everything. I didn't see either of them till it was all over for an hour or so." And with one last wild look around he headed for the door, only to come back to hold me to him for a brief moment as he whispered, "I love you baby, I'll go like the wind and be back before you know it...wake Jon if you need something." And then he was gone and I was left wondering if I had waited too long as another pain began to build. I couldn't help moaning aloud, and soon Jon was peeking in the door with wide eyes.

"Mother, what is it? Is it time for the baby to come? Where is Father?" "Don't worry, Jonny," I tried to reassure him, "He just left to get the doctor, they'll be back soon. You go back to sleep. I'll be all right till they get here." "But I don't want to leave you alone, let me just sit here by you, and keep you company," "Oh Jon, you are such a good boy, all right then, why don't you get a book and read aloud to me to pass the time, would you mind doing that?"

And that's how the doctor and Charlie found us, me tossing and turning in agony, trying not to scream out loud and Jon reading doggedly from one of his history books and wiping the sweat from both our faces with a wet cloth every few minutes as he was determined not to leave me.

The rest of the night is just a dim memory, but I do recall seeing the eastern sky begin to lighten and that was all until I heard Charlie's voice as from far, far away. It sounded like he was weeping, but why would Charlie be weeping? I could hear his words but couldn't understand what he was saying. I didn't want to wake up; it was too comfortable here where there was no pain so I drifted off somewhere again. When I heard voices again they were further away still, but I could hear them plainly..."I'm afraid we are losing her, there was just too much hemorrhaging." I strained to hear who they were talking about as it seemed to matter a great deal, then I heard my husband's voice close to my ear, and knew I had to stay and listen to him. So I concentrated hard and tried to open my eyes but they wouldn't, instead I just lay still and listened to Charlie bargaining with God. Why is he doing that? He knows you can't bargain with God. "Please Lord, don't take her from me, I can't stand it. I'll be a better person, I'll do anything You want, just don't let her slip away from me." Then I listened closer as his voice changed to an angry whisper in my ear, "Margaret, listen to me! Open your eyes and look at me! Don't you dare leave me alone with a baby to raise. I can't go through that again, I just can't!" Then his tone turned pleading again..."Please Maggie, open your eyes...don't you want to see our son? Come on now, be a good girl and we'll bring him to you." Then I felt a soft squirmy something being laid beside me and my hand was moved so I could touch it. At that first touch, sensation began flowing back into my limbs, and I could feel pain again, but now I didn't want to drift away from it. I fought to open my eyes and at last I could see Charlie's face, wet with tears leaning over me.

# Chapter 23

Spring had arrived at last, and I was dozing fitfully outdoors in the sunshine on a makeshift couch Charlie had fixed up for me. Recovery had taken an exasperatingly long time, and I was tired of being an invalid, but it seemed I could not regain my strength. Our baby was thriving and growing fat on his bottle of goat's milk that the doctor had advised for his feeding since I had no milk to nurse him. A hired girl helped to take care of the baby and the house and even do most of the cooking. I felt useless, utterly useless, and not even Charlie's teasing could bring me out of the depths of despair I felt at times.

Our son finally had a name thanks to his brother. For two weeks he was only known as Baby as we had no name chosen for a boy, so certain we had been of him being a girl. At last Charlie asked Jon what he thought he should be named, and his answer had been without hesitation "David." "Well," his father said blinking in surprise, "That's a good name, but why did you choose it? Sounds like you had it in your mind for awhile." "Why, don't you know about Jonathan and David from the Bible?" he replied, looking at his father questioningly. "I think that's how we will be. I'll always look after him and try not to let anything bad happen to him." His words made me realize again what an extraordinary boy Jon was. I held my hand out to him as he knelt at my bedside. I told him how much I loved him and brushed the hair out of his blue eyes. "Yes," I whispered, "David he will be. David Charles Preston, that will be a name he can be proud of."

Reverend Michaels came to the house for the baptism, and Sofie and Luke were there. Afterwards Sofie fussed around me like a mother hen. "If only we lived closer I could be here helpin' out. How I'd love to care for that li'l one in there, and you too. You jest rest till ya get strength back. Takes 'while to build up all the blood ya lost again I reckon..." "I don't know what's wrong with me," I replied wearily, "I just feel like a wet dish rag all the time."

So here it was nearly summer and I was still not myself. I knew I was being a worry to Charlie even though he tried not to show it. He had the doctor come and poke and prod me over more than once, but he had no answer to give except an abrupt, "She's just all run down from the ordeal and it takes time."

One morning in May while I was dragging wearily around the house in my wrapper after giving David his bottle, a buggy drove into the yard. I looked out the window and saw Sofie tie her mare to the gatepost and stride purposefully up the walk. I opened the door for her in surprise and asked what was wrong that she was here this time of day and on a weekday besides. She looked me over disgustedly, "I come to take ya for a ride on this beautiful day, and look atcha! What a sight! Get cleaned up and put on somethin' decent, and you'll feel better jest doin' that. Missy here can take care of David by herself for awhile, cantcha?" she asked the hired girl. "Of course I can take care of him," she answered drawing herself up proudly. "I been takin' care of babies since I was nine, I guess I can manage for awhile by myself." Missy's Dakotah name was Wah-CHA-ze which meant Sunflower, and a beautiful name, but we had all called her Missy since she was a baby.

Anyway when Sofie took that tone with me, I knew it was time to pay attention, and I did as she said. I took a bath in a hurry, combed my hair and put on a dress that would fit. I hadn't quite gotten my figure back since David's birth, so had been wearing loose floppy things around the house not caring much what I looked like. Just the thought of being with Sofie cheered me up a bit and when I glanced in the mirror, I thought I looked more like my old self than I had for months.

"All right now, that's a mite better!" She grinned as I came out of the bedroom with my pan of bath water to throw over the back yard fence. "Here, I'll get rid o' that for ya, don't wantcha spillin' all over that nice dress."

So she took me for a ride in her buggy, the horse just at a walk, meandering through the meadows of the foothills where the wildflowers were beginning to bloom. The warm sun on my face and the fresh green smell of the new grass was as good as a spring tonic. Looking east across the valley was refreshing and made me remember how I used to feel when I would look at this beautiful land that was Roberts County.

Under a tree that was nearly leafed out, Sofie pulled the buggy to a stop, looped the reins and turned to look me straight in the eye. "Now, s'pose you tell me what's ailin' ya? And don't be givin' me the old song an' dance 'bout takin' a long time to get strong again. Your husband, bless his heart, is worried plumb sick 'bout you. He made a special trip over to ask if I'd talk to ya. I'da been here sooner if I'd known what a state you've gotten yourself into but I din't know...Why didn't ya send me a postcard or somethin'?"

I had to turn away from that piercing gaze that could see to the depths of my soul. Staring out across the valley I tried to put into words how I felt and it wasn't easy. "Oh Sofie, I have never been afraid of life before. I've always been able to pick up and keep going, and wouldn't you think now that we have a new son to care for I would be anxious to get on with it? But I'm so terribly afraid...afraid we're too old and something will happen to us before David is grown, and then what will become of him? I'm going to be an old woman if I do live to see him be twenty-one, and think of Charlie! He's ten years older than me even!" And with that I burst into wrenching sobs that shook the buggy and started the mare to prancing about so Sofie had to quiet her.

"Well, honestly! I never heard of sech a dumb thing to be afraid of. What's the matter with you anyway? Come on now, quitcher cryin', you're scarin' Betty. She ain't used to bawlin' females." She put her arms around me awkwardly and patted me on the back, "There, there, maybe its best if ya do get it all outa your system, then you'll be able to think plainer and make some sense." And she sat quietly patting me until I finally began to get control of myself and could turn to face her again. "I'm afraid too, that I'm going crazy, and might never be able to have a normal life again. Remember that woman who lived out in the township at Travare? She just sat and stared at nothing most of the time, what if I would get like that?" "Oh fiddlesticks!" Sofie scoffed, "What's wrong with you is nothin' like what was wrong with that pore soul. Lotsa women feel down and out for a long time after they have a baby. I'm s'prised yore doctor din't say as much. He sure musta seen it before. I know I have plenty o' times. Why I remember when Ben was born, there I was, nothin' but a green girl...with a new baby, husband to feed, washin' to do, felt like my feet was made o' lead, draggin' round tryin' to do everthing alone and scared to death of doin' somethin' wrong with the baby...Finally, my ol' Granny took me in hand. She come and helped out what she could, but the main thing was she made me feel like I could manage again. It was all jest in my head."

"I know you had a bad time of it, and we coulda lost you, but most us women are tough, tougher than men, probly, if the truth was known. Besides, don't you be wastin' time worryin' 'bout what's to come. That's in the Lord's hands and nothin' we can do 'bout it but pray for strength to go on ahead. You and Charlie are healthy as hounds and likely gonna live to see a dozen grand babies anyhow!" Sofie laughed in her old happy way, and took up the reins again. "Now, how 'bout you makin' us a cuppa coffee when we get back, and let me set and rock my little Davey for awhile?"

## CHAPTER 24

Back in town, Abigail thanked Martha for showing her around the cemetery, and said that she would pass on lunch today as the street was lined on both sides with pickup trucks, so the café was probably full. She got back in her car and drove slowly through the town's few streets wondering where Charlie and Maggie's house had been. But she had no way of knowing at that time, so eventually headed east out into the countryside, looking for Travare.

It was easy to find the site, and she pulled the car onto an approach to a cornfield and got out to look around. The fields where once had been a town were all planted now, but she walked along the road looking to the east where she thought the courthouse would have stood. "Why can't there be a magic potion that could take me back and let me see what it looked like then!" She muttered in frustration...Martha had said the farm house was on the foundation of Sofie and Luke's hotel, so that gave her a sense of how the town had been laid out, with this road being the main street. Probably houses or stores along both sides. The schoolhouse would have been farther out in the country, and where would Grandpa Charlie's store building have been? It was a mystery and likely to remain one, as very few pictures had been found of Travare she had been told.

So at last, with a sigh, she got back in the car and drove slowly down the hill into the town of Browns Valley. It was an odd feeling, driving down the hill where over a hundred years ago her grandma and grandpa would have ridden in the buggy and sleigh. There was the big log cabin that Maggie had written about and she pulled up, parked across the street and looked at it in amazement. It was odd, but Abigail was more impressed with these fairly recent things of history than she had been the first time she had been to Market Street in Philadelphia. The cabin appeared to be open for visitors so she walked up to the door and peeked in. "Come on in, we're open!" a voice called from within. A grandmotherly looking woman was behind a desk in the next room, and she began her explanation by pointing out the pictures of J.R. and Samuel J. Brown, Chief Renville and some of the many relics of the late 1800s. Among them Sam Brown's wheel chair and desk. Out in the next rooms were pictures of pioneers of the area and Abigail wandered through the door and began to scan them quickly looking at names as she went.

From the other room the attendant heard a squeal of delight and smiled to herself. It was a happy bonus of her volunteer job at the cabin when young people took an interest in the history of the area. With a face radiant with her discovery Abigail bounced out of the back room and announced with glee, "I found my Grandpa Charlie on one of these pictures! Come and see!" She pointed to one of four dignified looking gentlemen in dark suits standing soberly for a portrait. "See? There he is! C.B. Preston, County Commissioner, Roberts County, D.T. 1883." She pointed to the tallest of the men who although he was as unsmiling as the others, looked as if he might have a twinkle of mirth in his clear eyes. "Oh-h," the older woman sighed, "He was a handsome devil wasn't he?" and grinned at Abigail. "Wasn't he though? I can see why Grandma Maggie carried a torch for him for eleven years. This is a wonderful place! So tell me more about Sam and Phoebe Brown."

# CHAPTER 25

**May 1904...Peever**

Another spring! Everything was bursting into to life again after a long cold winter. I had just finished my spring house cleaning. It was a pleasure instead of work cleaning our lovely new house. Charlie remembered that he had promised to build us a new house back in 1884 when he first asked me to marry him. "Finally got the job done Maggie, only about twenty years late!" He had exclaimed last October as we stood outside admiring the front of the house with its wrap around porch and frosted glass in the door. Then without warning he scooped me in his arms and carried me up the steps, and as David opened the door for us he carried me through into the front hall with its beautiful oak floor.

"Charlie you fool! What will the neighbors think!" I hissed as he set me down at last in our spacious parlor. "Since when, my dearest Maggie, have you cared a hoot what the neighbors or anyone else thought?" he retorted with that wicked twinkle in his eye, "Besides no one is looking unless Mrs. Peterson is peeking out from behind her lace curtains."

I had gotten used to the idea of living in town again, and rather liked the convenience and having neighbors close by. And the best part of all...Charlie had his own business again. He had started to publish the *Peever Weekly* just last year and was the sole owner and editor in chief. He built his building on the west side of main street, and there was plenty of room for all the equipment needed to print a newspaper. He was much happier being his own boss, being free to voice his own opinions on politics or town issues as he pleased.

Another advantage of moving to town was that now we lived six miles closer to Sofie and Luke, as their farm was just two miles east of Peever. We could see each other almost every weekend, as they came into town for the church services that were held in the school and homes.

Sofie and Luke had built onto their house that spring of 1890, and then she had a kitchen table big enough to feed a family of ten or hold a side of beef at butchering time. Of course they didn't have a family of ten, but Ben, Helena, and their two children took the train from

Corona fairly often. Then they either walked to the farm, hired a rig, or Charlie and I would take them out there. Ben was the same good hearted person he always was. He and I usually had a lot to talk about, sharing our teaching experiences.

Peever was a booming little city that year of 1904. Main Sreet was lined on both sides with businesses and many on the side streets as well. Stores, elevators, livery barns, banks, hotels, eating places, saloons and pool halls, a lumberyard. Mr. Peever had a good idea starting his town here, even though it was on the edge of a slough. There was a muddy mess in the streets and yards that year with the spring rains. But by summer it had dried and except for the ruts that were left, getting around was much easier.

I found a bag and put in my rolling pin, an apron, and five pounds of white flour. Four other women and I were going to make lefse. "David!" I called as I was starting to leave, "Where are you? I'm ready to go." He came out from behind the house dragging his feet. "Aw Ma, do I have to go with you? I'd rather stay home alone." "Well, you can't stay home alone, and that's that, so come on, we have a lot to do today." "Why can't I go to the print office with Dad and Jon instead? I don't wanna be with a whole buncha women all day." He put on the sulky face that could annoy his father and I so much, but his brown eyes looked up at me with the pleading gaze that I found hard to resist. "Oh all right! But I will walk with you part way to make sure you get there. I don't want you playing around on the tracks and in the street again. The train is due in another half hour." So I took my son by the hand and went with him until we could see Charlie's building a block away. Then I told him to run straight there while I watched. When he was at the door he turned and waved to me as he went in.

As I walked on to Myra Jensen's house in the north part of town I thought about David. Five years old this March. He was beginning to learn his letters and would be soon reading simple things. "Lord, help me not to spoil this son of mine," I prayed as I walked along. It would be easy to do, as he was a much more headstrong child than Jon had ever been. He idolized his big brother and Jon took the promise seriously that he had made when David was a baby, to watch over him whenever he could.

With my children on my mind I was at the door of Myra's house before I knew it and found the other women in the kitchen all ready, rolling and frying lefse at a great rate, while their cheerful chatter filled the room. We were preparing for the May 17th celebration that the town observed in honor of Syttend Mai, or Norwegian

Independence Day. It was a day of fun and games, horse races, foot races, sack races, tug of war and speeches, but mostly just people enjoying a day off work in the middle of the week after a long winter. Our church group was selling lunches and we liked to have some of the traditional Norwegian food, therefore the lefse making. At Milda Jensen's place another group was making rosettes and fattigman. Sofie had volunteered to make the fruit soup and would bring it along when she and Luke came to town in the morning. "Yah, and here's Maggie at last, ve vere vondering if you were gonna get here or if that goot looking man of joors kept you home with him today." Myra teased in her thick Norwegian brogue. "Here now, iss a spot for you to roll out, I'll yust move over a bit." As I tied on my apron and sprinkled flour on the table to roll my first lefse, my thoughts went back to the early days in Travare when I took cooking lessons from Sofie everyday and slowly learned how to put a meal together. I had to smile at the memories as I let the talk of the others go over my head, and relived some of those times.

"You are very quiet today Maggie," remarked Mrs. Barton, the banker's wife, from across the table. She had been a girl from Boston, and married a man who was determined to go west and get in on the starting of a new town. "Just remembering some things," I answered. "When I first came to Dakota Territory, I didn't know the first thing about cooking and baking. We always had hired help to do that. I can't believe how ignorant I was." "I know, it was about the same with me at home." Melinda replied, as she began rolling another ball of lefse dough. "A cook in the kitchen and maids upstairs and down to do everything. When we came here, I thought I had come to the ends of the earth, but soon learned how to manage, as I had no other choice."

The Norwegians, Swedes and Danes outnumbered the rest of the white people here in Peever and surrounding area. Charlie and I were both from Scottish-English descent, and we were among the minority. The Bartons, were English too, so Melinda and I had that in common as well.

We worked mostly in silence then, hurrying to get as much done as we could. Myra set on a pot of water to make coffee, and announced that when it was ready we were going to sit down and rest and sample our lefse. There was another bowl of mashed potatoes cooling until the flour could be mixed in. "What you tink Maggie? Duss this look like it's going to be enuff?" Louisa Swenson asked as she waved floury hands over the stacks waiting to be folded in fourths and packaged until tomorrow. "Well, I remember last year we made 200, and we sold nearly all, so have you been counting? How many is that?" I answered. "One hunret twenty five, iff I counted right," Louisa said, while flipping another off the griddle expertly. "If ve do up that last bowl of potatoes, ve should have plenty then, I should tink unless there's a lot bigger crowd this year. Ya, ve yust never know, but not effrybody eats lefse anyhow."

"Vonder who all's gonna race their horses this year?" Myra wondered. "I yust luff a good horse race. Takes me back when I wass young and the boys wud race effry chance they got. Joor man gonna race hiss big black devil of a horse Maggie?" "No," I answered, "Charlie said he was leaving the racing to the younger fellows from now on. But I think Jon might ride that pinto he bought from the trader that came through a few months ago."

That night as we lay in bed, I asked Charlie something that had been on my mind lately. I had noticed Jonathan had become quieter and more withdrawn the last few months. Sometimes I caught him staring out the window looking west toward the hills as the sun went down, and wondered what was on his mind. So now I asked his father, "What do you think Jon wants to do with his life now that he is nearly grown?" Charlie jumped a little at the question and turned to look at me, raising on his elbow, "Why? Don't you think he wants to stay here? I just thought...he seems to like working on the paper, that he'd just take it over in a few years. Wouldn't that be nice...to have our son take over the business and carry it on?" "Yes dear, there's nothing that would please me better, but we have to find out what he really wants Charlie, you and I can't decide his future by what we would like." Charlie sighed heavily, and lay down again with his face half in the pillow as he mumbled, "I know, I know, It's all been wishful thinking on my part, I just hate to think of him going away. He's so smart, I suppose he should go to college somewhere, I wonder if he would want to study the law?" "Well," I said, trying to sound brisk but with a lump in my throat at the sadness in Charlie's voice, "You talk to him about it when you are alone, and find out what he thinks...after the celebration is over and it's quiet around here again. Sometimes he looks like he has something on his mind, but he never says a thing about it to me."

I stood watching the races the next day from the doorway of the building where we had the food stand. Everyone was outside anyway, cheering on their favorite so there was nothing to do. They would come back in again for more lunch when the races were over. Jonathan was a handsome sight riding his pinto bareback, his black hair blowing in the wind. I watched the young girls on the sidelines clapping as he rode by, and thought, "Oh yes, all of you think my son is wonderful, but what would your parents say if you told them you wanted to marry Jonathan Preston?" To many he was still "That half breed boy of Charlie's." I bit my lip in anger as these thoughts surfaced and I tried to put them away, so as not to spoil my day. In all honesty, I couldn't blame the white settlers and townspeople. When they came here many of them had never so much as seen an Indian, and some still had the idea they were living among savages. It had been so different for Charlie and me as we had, from the start, been involved in the lives of the Dakotah people.

After the winners were announced, the crowd scattered and we had a few more hungry people wanting another cup of coffee and a doughnut, ham sandwich, or just one more lefse with butter and sugar. I had no more time to think about Jon as we were kept busy until 6:00 with cleaning the building and putting everything away.

A dance was being held in the loft over the grocery store, beginning at eight, so I hurried home to see how my family was doing and make sure that everyone got dressed and ready to go. David had been having fun all day with the games and watching the goings on, and he would be tired and fall asleep early. But the children went along to our dances usually, and we just put down blankets behind the chairs for them to lay when they got sleepy.

Jon was already home when I got there but he was just sitting at the kitchen table in the clothes he had worn all day, reading a map. When I came through the door he hastily folded it as if not wanting me to see. "Jonny," I asked hesitantly, "Aren't you going to get changed for the dance?" looking at him closely to see what was going on in his head. But as usual, he shut me out with a smile, and answered, "I didn't think I would go this time, I'll just stay home with David if you want. Then you and Father can enjoy yourselves without having to keep an eye on him."

"But we don't want to go without you two, and why on earth would you want to stay home? The girls will be waiting for you to ask them to dance I'm sure." At this he looked down, and shuffled his feet uncomfortably under the table as he mumbled, "I don't think their folks like it when they dance with me and anyway I'm not very good at it." I hated to see the hurt look in his eyes and ignoring the first part of his reason for not going I tackled the second.

"Come on now Jon, let's have a dance lesson. Your father should have done this, he's the one who can really dance well, but I will try.

We'll put a record on the gramaphone and have a waltz first, then do something else. Hurry up now!"

When Charlie came home he heard the music coming from the parlor and stuck his head in to see what was going on. He leaned against the doorframe watching until the song was over as Jon and I waltzed around the room. Clapping his hands at the end of the dance he smiled at us and said softly, "May I have the next one? I remember that first Christmas dance I took her to Jon, and she was the prettiest woman there. Had to do some fast talking to get her to go with me, but she eventually gave in." Jonathan laughed as he stepped aside and went to restart the record. "Go ahead, you two, I'm going up to change clothes."

It was a jolly evening with the floor crowded with happy couples and the chatter and music filled the room. David went to sleep early as I suspected he would, along with several of the younger children. Charlie and I were sitting out a couple of dances visiting with Myra and Sven when Jon and Mary Barton went by. Mary was a picture pretty sixteen-year-old whose blonde head just came to Jon's shoulder. She was staring up at him with what could only be called the calf-eyed look, as my parents used to say. Jon was guiding her around the floor in good form and as he passed by gave us a smile . Charlie poked me in the ribs and remarked, "Those lessons of yours must have given Jon the confidence he needed." "That's all he needed too, he knows the steps perfectly," I answered, "He just was feeling down in the mouth about something tonight when we got home."

No sooner were the words out, than across the room I saw the son of the grocery store owner cut in on Jon, and waltz away with Mary. Then he turned and mouthed something that made Jon's face turn a dull red and his eyes flash in anger. With balled up fists, he turned and walked off the floor and out the door. I looked at Charlie, and he rose and followed him into the street. I sat as if turned to stone because I had read the other's lips and knew the insulting name he had called our son..."Jonny, Jonny, I'm so sorry, but nothing we can say is going to make it any better for you." This thought lay like lead in my stomach as the music and talk swirled around me. I had lost all interest in the evening and only wanted to gather my family and go home, but waited until Charlie came back in alone and looked down at me soberly. "Ready to call it a night Maggie? I'll pick Davey up and carry him so he will stay asleep." As we said goodnight to the Peterson's I tried to keep a smile on my face, in hopes they hadn't noticed anything amiss, and followed Charlie out the door into the cool dark night. As we walked, he told me that Jon had bolted down the street for home by the time he had gotten outside.

After we had put David to bed, we stopped in front of the closed door of Jon's room and looked at each other uncertainly. Charlie raised his hand to knock, then put it down again. I nodded to him and whispered, "I think you should talk to him yet tonight." "You come with me then," he pleaded, "I don't know if I'll say the right thing, I'll maybe just mess everything up worse." I nodded again and squeezed his arm, "You'll do fine, but I'll go in if that's what you want." There was silence after Charlie's hesitant knock, and we waited until we heard a muffled "Come in." Jon was stretched out on the bed, still dressed with his arm flung across his face. Charlie sat on the edge of the bed and put a hand on his son's shoulder, "Do you feel like talking Jon? Your mother and I are worried about you. We saw what happened, and are proud that you didn't start a fight over it."

At this Jon opened his eyes, sat up, and said in a rush, "It's always going to be like that here. I know it will. I want to go away. I've been thinking, I'd like to go west and find where I was born and see my Mother's people." I couldn't help a startled jump at those words, and Jon looked at me with painful apology in his eyes as he continued, "I guess what I really want to do is be a missionary and go there and teach them about Jesus." If Jon had said he wanted to be an acrobat in the circus, Charlie could not have looked more stunned. He sat staring at his son as if he had never seen him before while his mouth hung open in dismay. As for me, it was no great surprise. I had seen from the beginning where Jon's interests were, and if Charlie had been more observant he would have noticed it too.

I took Charlie's hand in mind and smiled at Jon in what I hoped was encouragement, "Well! It might take your father some time to get used to this idea, and do you know there will be years of study before you qualify for the ministry? Are you sure you want that?" He looked up at me hopefully, as Charlie still had not spoken, "Do you think I really could? I know it will cost a lot, can we afford it?" I shook Charlie's arm to bring him around and asked, "So what do you think about it? I still have some of the inheritance left from when Mother died. We didn't use any of that to build the house or start the business, so why can't it go for the seminary? It certainly couldn't be put to a better use, in my idea." I was talking just to get Charlie started even if he was going to have a conniption fit, as Sofie would call it. But he didn't have a fit. He shook his head like a bull that had run into the barn wall by mistake, but rallied bravely and tried to smile as he watched his dreams for Jon disappear into the mountains of Montana.

## CHAPTER 26

Abigail parked the car beside the old church that stood in front of a fenced in cemetery near the Agency. It was a still June afternoon with the bees hovering around the wild roses that bloomed beside the roadway. She breathed deeply of the pure country air and looked up at the hills that were so close that she could see the green slopes and the deeper green of the oak trees in the coulees. What a gorgeous place, no wonder Grandma Maggie loved it out here, she thought.

As she walked slowly through the cemetery gate she noticed an old man pulling weeds around some of the graves by the north fence. He straightened up from his work as she approached and greeted her with a smile. "Good afternoon! Can I help you with something?" He tossed his handful of weeds over the fence and came closer to look her in the face. He brushed the dirt onto his trousers and held out a gnarled brown hand. "I'm Reverend GreyElk, and who might you be?" Smiling back at this friendly preacher Abigail told him her name and that she came from the east to find family records. "Well," he told her, "I have been here for fifty odd years since I moved from Minnesota, and have been the minister of this church for nearly thirty of those years. Some days are pretty quiet, and I pass the time looking into the history of this church. I've hunted through the early records many times, so maybe I can help you. Come inside with me and we'll have a look. It might take awhile, but I have tried to keep things in order by the years."

Abigail followed the elderly man into the tiny white church that appeared to be very old from the interior furnishings and uneven wooden floor. "Watch your step," he warned as he walked into the room at the left side of the sanctuary. "The floor is bad here, something has to be done about this, but no one has gotten at it yet. Now," he continued, "What years are you looking for and what are the names?" So she told him of Charlie and Maggie's marriage in 1896, and that she wasn't certain this was the right church, but according to Maggie's writing it appeared to likely. "Ah yes, that would have been during Jacob Michaels' years, not long after the church was built." "Reverend Michaels!" Abigail exclaimed happily, "That's the one! He was mentioned several times in her diaries, and I know he married them and baptized the baby David." She looked eagerly over his shoulder as he laid an ancient book on the desk and began to thumb through the closely written pages.

"See," Reverend GreyElk pointed out, "Marriages and baptisms are on separate pages so we don't have to wade through everything. That will make it easier." Running his finger down the pages he soon found the year and the month and there it was in black and white...Married 30 June, 1896...Charles B. Preston, and Margaret Sinclair Marshall. Witnessed by Lucas Johnson and Sofia Johnson. Abigail bit her lip to hide the emotion she felt at finding one more written record that these people actually lived and breathed. She traced the thin spidery handwriting of the long ago Reverend Michaels with her finger and blinked to clear her eyes of the film that covered them. Turning to the old man she asked huskily, "And the baptisms? They are in this book too?" "Right on this next page," he answered turning it over carefully, and smoothing it down. "David wasn't born until two years later, so we'll have to go further." But just then a name jumped up at her from the page...Jonathan B. (M'ne-Ska ) Preston...baptized 18 July 1896. "Of course! Jon wouldn't have been baptized before as they lived in the wilds of Montana where there was no Christian Church yet. According to grandma, Jon went to the seminary and became a missionary, going back to Montana to find his mother's people. His mother was Sioux, but from Montana," she explained. "Ah yes," the old one said softly looking into the distance, "Now that I see that name again I recall hearing the story of the young blue eyed missionary, who had at one time been in the Sunday School at this church."

Abigail caught her breath in surprise at the Reverend's words, "What do you mean? I have no idea what became of him. Grandma's diary mentioned that he had died, but, he is not by her and Charlie in the Peever cemetery." The creased brown face puckered into a thoughtful frown as he replied, "No, he would not be there, his remains were never found, although it broke his father and mother's heart they say, not being able to bury their son." "Oh no!" Abigail cried, "Why? What happened to him? What do you mean he was never found?"

The old man sighed and answered, "Come, let's go across to my house and I'll make a cup of tea. I could use a break, and you look a little frazzled. I'll tell you what I know of the story while we are sitting down. My old legs don't like to be standing around too long anymore." He chuckled in amusement as he joked, "My congregation doesn't mind though, because they know my sermons won't last more than fifteen minutes."

The tea was good and hot and strong, just what she needed to "put the starch back in her" as Sofie would have said, and Abigail settled back to listen the Reverend GreyElk's account of Jonathan.

"You know," he began, "My people have always loved a good story and will make a legend out of a heroic person and retell it over and over. I heard this when I first came to Roberts County and the story stayed the same so I never doubted that it was true...Apparently someone from the tribe in Montana came here and told about the young man who had been full of the Great Spirit or as we would say the Holy Spirit. They called him by his tribal name M'ne-Ska which means White Water, and in his short life he brought many people to Christ out of the old religion. More tea miss?" He asked, as he pushed back his chair. "Let me," Abigail said quickly, rising to get the pot off the stove. "You go on with the story. Then what happened?" He stirred two heaping teaspoons of sugar into his cup before continuing slowly. "The mountain streams in Montana can be very treacherous. They rush down out of the gorges into narrow spaces where the water boils over the rocks, which is how he got his name in the first place, I suppose, as his mother was from there. Yes, that is very likely," he murmured softly as he thought how to continue. "Well, the way I understand it, a child from the village had taken a canoe out by himself to try to prove to his father how grown up he was, as children will, you know, and had gotten himself upset in a rough part of the river. He was hanging on to the overturned canoe and the current was sweeping him away toward the rocks when M'ne-Ska jumped in after him. The young missionary was tall and strong, and managed to fling the boy out of the current into the waters closer to shore where his father could reach him. But the white water swept the preacher away and he was never seen again."

Abigail sat in silence digesting this sorrowful tale feeling real grief for the lost Jonathan who had meant so much to Charlie and Maggie. "Why did I come to South Dakota?" she asked herself sadly. "I didn't want to know all this stuff, and I surely didn't want it to matter this much. All I wanted was to find out some family history." Reverend GreyElk looked at her with his wise old eyes and understood what she was feeling somehow as he said quietly, "I haven't told you the end of the legend...The family of the boy that was saved had been opposed to the blue-eyed preacher's message and tried to turn the village against him, even so far as plotting to have him killed. When they saw how he had given his life for their son, they turned to Christianity and their entire family was baptized, and eventually the heads of the families went around the other remote villages spreading the Word. It's an inspiring story don't you think?" Abigail looked up from her tea cup that she had been staring into and gave him shaky smile. "It's a beautiful story, and what I have read of Jonathan, he would have been satisfied with the ending. According to Grandma Maggie he was a special child from the time he was very young." Rising slowly from her chair she held out her hand to the Reverend and smiled gently, "Thanks so much for everything...the tea...and telling me the story of Jonathan. I'll never forget it, and if I ever have children I'll be sure to tell them the legend of M'ne-Ska, our long ago ancestor."

# CHAPTER 27

July 1910...I was hanging out the washing that Monday morning when I saw a team and wagon round our corner at a gallop and pull into Dr. Murdoch's front yard. I thought I recognized Luke's horses from between the sheets I was trying to hang against the wind that blew strongly from the south. I put in the last pin and walked around the clothesline to see what was going on. To my horror I saw Sofie leaping off the seat calling as she did for the doctor. She ran to the back of the wagon and let down the endgate and I could see that something was covered with a blood soaked blanket. With cold dread seeping into my soul I ran across the yard just as Doc came out the door and hurried down the steps. I reached the wagon at the same time he pulled the blanket back, and as I got a look at what was underneath I closed my eyes as the sky began to tilt. Clutching the wheel to keep from falling, I took deep breaths to get my balance back. Sofie was kneeling in the wagon beside Luke's body, rubbing his lifeless hands, praying over and over in a hopeless chant, "Oh please God, Please, please, please, don't let him be daid, Oh God, please." Doc took her by the arms and helped her out as he spoke softly to her, "Here's Maggie, Sofie, stand by her for a minute while I have a look, all right?" He gave me a steely glare that said I had better pull myself together and not faint on him. I put my arms around Sofie's thin little body and held her close, but it was as if she didn't even know me as she kept on with her pitiful prayer.

The neighbors and townspeople gathered at our house where I had led Sofie while Luke was taken to the undertaking parlour. She was shaking with shock and her teeth chattering as if she were freezing even though the morning was already oppressively hot. I got a blanket out of the closet and wrapped her in it while she told what had happened through blue and trembling lips. Luke was breaking a wild bronco that he had bought from a trader who shipped the ponies in from Wyoming. Sofie had been watching from behind the fence and saw when he was thrown. In a split second the bronco had whirled and trampled him with its sharp hooves, crushing Luke's head and chest. Sofie ran for the shot gun, loaded it, and emptied the barrel into the pony...Somehow she got the horses hitched up and lifted the broken body of her husband into the wagon. Luke weighed almost twice as much as she, and I just shook my head as I thought of her determination to do what had to be done in the face of disaster. Would I ever be that strong? I did not think so.

I finally shooed everyone outside saying that Sofie needed to rest and have it quiet. By this time Charlie had gotten word and was sitting with us, his face ashen with shock and grief. David was hovering uncertainly on the sidelines knowing that he had to be still, but not fully realizing what was going on. I saw Charlie beckon him over, pull him close and whisper something to him. Our son had not yet experienced death so close to home. Of course others in Peever had died and been buried in the new cemetery south of town. Mr Peever's death two years ago touched everyone, but David was too young then to pay much attention, just knew that he was gone and never came to his store anymore.

Friends took care of the chores for Sofie, and Ben and his family came as soon as they could. We went with them to pick out a burying place for Luke. Sofie strode ahead of us to the far northeast corner and announced, "Here's where he'll be...next to the fields, not crowded in betweenst a bunch o'others." And that's how it was. His coffin was carried by Charlie and five other of his old friends from Travare, and as the hot July wind blew relentlessly, Lucas Johnson was laid to rest.

# CHAPTER 28

Abigail was parked beside the road picking wild roses on the way back to Peever. "Grandma's favorite wild flower, least I can do is lay some on their graves before I go, Ouch!" She yelped as a thorn stuck in her thumb. Sucking on the tiny puncture, she mumbled to herself, "Darn, I should have put on gloves to do this." But she kept on clipping the stems with her manicure scissors until she had a fine looking armfull. As she parked at the cemetery and gingerly gathered her bouquet off the seat she noticed another car parked outside the fence. Walking across to the northeast corner she saw a man kneeling by the four graves reading the names. He hadn't seen or heard her so she cleared her throat hesitantly and ventured a "Hello," to make him aware of her presence. He jumped a little in surprise and got to his feet. "Oh! I didn't expect anyone else to be here, I was trying to make out the dates, this marble weathers pretty badly until the inscriptions are nearly unreadable." He didn't look like he was one of the local men as he wore his suit and tie casually this weekday afternoon as if it was his usual dress. Abigail knelt to place the roses across all four of the graves before she replied curiously, "Are you looking for ancestors too? That's what brought me here." "Yes," he answered, "But actually, I knew they were buried here, although I haven't been back to Peever since I was a little boy with my parents. Sofie and Luke Johnson are my aunt and uncle, I don't even know how many greats." He laughed as he held out his hand, "Larry MacRae...from Minneapolis, and who are you?" Abigail shook his hand as she told him and the two young people eyed each other up and down in a quick appraisal of each other's good looks. Larry MacRae gave her a crooked grin while remarking, "This is quite the coincidence, meeting like this. What do you think of going to the café and having coffee while we share what we know about our families?"

Connie smiled to herself as she saw the two with their heads together, reading Maggie's diaries and chattering away in the corner booth. She knew who Larry was as he had stopped for lunch before going to the cemetery, and they had struck up a conversation by the cash register. Connie never lost an opportunity to visit with strangers when they gave the least indication of wanting to talk. She had found out that he was junior vice president of a brokerage company in the cities, on his way back from meeting with a client in Aberdeen, single and interested in family history. That last fact alone made him an O.K. person in Connie's estimation.

"What a character my aunt Sofie must have been." Larry remarked after reading the portions that Abigail pointed out to him. "Yes, and a true friend always. She and grandma remained close throughout the years even though they lived some miles apart back when it wasn't easy to travel."

But time was ticking away, and at last, with a look at her watch, Abigail sighed in regret and said that she would have to leave for Watertown. Her suitcases were packed and in the car and all she had to do was say goodbye to Connie, Bill and Jeanne. Larry stood reluctantly and watched as she put her things back into the tote bag. "Listen," he said urgently, "Let's not lose track of each other. Here's my card, it's got everything on it...phone number...E-Mail address, call me when you get back to Philadelphia, will you? Or..." and he stopped in confusion. "You have someone back there waiting for you no doubt, I'm maybe being presumptuous." Abigail laughed to ease his discomfort and replied, "No, there is no one waiting for me except my boss, my family, and an independent cat. I haven't found the man yet who could put up with my notions." She took a napkin out of the holder, scribbled an address and phone number, folded it and stuck it in his pocket. "There now, you call ME when you get back to Minneapolis if you still feel like it. I'm just old fashioned enough to think the man should make the first move!" She gave him a wink as they shook hands then said their goodbyes to Connie. As she backed the rental car out carefully, Abigail called out, "Be sure to watch for the kids, they use Main Street for a playground!"

## Chapter 29

**July 1911**

Luke had been dead for a year when Sofie came to me with her proposition. "Margret," she announced that morning over coffee in my kitchen, "I went an' sold th' farm. What do you think o' that?" I stirred my coffee thoughtfully before answering, "It's really the only sensible thing for you to do, I would think. Having to hire all the help must eat up a lot of the profit doesn't it?" "I know, but I sure hated t' sell it when it was Luke's pride n' joy, that place. He'd did so much work fixin' it up. Leastways its done and no turnin' back. Now I gotta do somethin' diff'rent." She got up and filled our cups from the pot on the cookstove while I waited for what she would say. She sat down again and looked out the window for a minute or two before continuing. "You probly know the big hotel and eatin' place next t' the dry goods store is bein' sold? The folks is goin' back east I hear. Anyways I spoke to 'em 'bout it already, an' we purty much agreed on th' price. So what I was thinkin'...you n' me would make a purty good pair at runnin' it...don'tcha think so?" She finished in a hurry watching for my reaction. Well, that was the last thing I expected to hear and sat speechless, staring at Sofie while she leaned back and eyed me carefully. "Ya know, I could hire somebody I s'pose, but a partner would be better, and I jest thought since yer boy is gettin' bigger and don't need ya so much anymore, you could probly use somethin' t' spend yer time on. Whatta ya say?" I replied hesitantly and in some confusion, "Sofie, I just don't know what to say. For the first thing, I don't have hardly any money left since we drew out almost everything to send Jon to the seminary. For another thing, I can't imagine what Charlie would say about it. I know he likes having me at home when he gets finished working and I like having his meals ready on time..." I finished lamely. "Oh hogwash!" Sofie burst out, "As if Charlie would ever stand in yer way if there was somethin' you really wanted t'do. But if ya don't wanna I guess I'd understand. It would be hard work, fer sure. But a good money maker. I never said I wanted you to put cash money in, I got that. I jus need someone I can trust t'help with the plannin', keepin' track o' the books and stuff. At Travare, Luke, rest his soul, did the writin' down fer me, as I wern't much good at it. We can hire a girl or two to help with the washin' and cleanin' and stuff. As far as Charlie goes, him and Davey can jest run 'cross th' street and have their dinner with us when we're done with th' customers, and we'll fix it so you can get home before supper time. One o' the girls'l stay an' help for later."

She finally stopped to draw breath while gazing at me shrewdly, then went on, "I kinda had the feelin' that a little extra money might come in handy for you and Charlie." I couldn't help feeling a little embarrassed and knew my face had turned red at realizing Sofie knew Charlie and I were having a hard time making ends meet. Expenses at the printing office had nearly doubled. Subscribers were unwilling to pay higher rates and the paper was simply not making what we planned. The house wasn't all paid for yet which meant extra interest had piled up...Charlie had almost lost his carefree grin and too often it was replaced with a worried frown when he thought I wasn't watching. I had thought of going back to work, but didn't know what. Married women just didn't teach school here, and I couldn't think what else to do. Charlie had even started bartending at the saloon in the evenings sometimes. Or during the day when he was done at the office he would help out the dray man or at the livery barn. David worked at odd jobs when he wasn't in school, but the money just never seemed to reach.

Sofie leaned over and patted my hand gently, "Don't feel bad Margret, everybody comes on hard times some time r' other. I din't mean t' embarrass ya. If we did do this, we could be helpin' each other outa a pinch. 'Member how you n me used t' work together purty good in the old days? I think on those times a lot and th' fun I had teachin' ya how to cook. Those were happy days back then fer th' most part, wern't they? Ya know, we shoulda been able t' keep that town together even without the courthouse seems like, but everbody pulled out so fast." Then she shook her head and sighed, "All water over th' bridge now anyhow. This is a good town too, we jest gotta have jobs to be keepin' people here. I'm always scairt Charlie will take in his head to move west again, I sure would hate t'see ya all move away."

"Oh no, I'm sure he isn't thinking about starting over anywhere else. But it has gotten to be a struggle lately. Maybe I will take you up on your offer even though it doesn't seem quite fair to you. But I'm not long on pride these days Sofie, and if I can help Charlie get things back on an even footing again, I would be grateful. Thank you dear friend, for thinking of us, and I will certainly do my best to help make it work."

**April 1915...**
Sofie and I stood helplessly from two blocks away watching the west side of main street become a raging inferno. It had begun around 2:00 AM they said, and every able bodied man was fighting to keep the flames from spreading across the street. The roof of Charlie's printing office had all ready fallen in and a garage and implement business south of there were beyond help also. The flames from the bank building and grocery store shot skyward, sparks flying everywhere against the dark sky. It was a fearful sight. We stood and prayed for the men who were fighting, that their lives would be spared, but selfishly all I could think of were Charlie and David. We had lost our beloved Jonathan that spring, and I had felt we couldn't stand anything more, now this. Oh my poor Charlie, I mourned, as tears ran unchecked down my face. The buildings on the east side of the street seemed to be escaping so far. Our hotel with its double porches could be seen plainly from where we stood, and the dry goods store next to it was still standing so we gave thanks for that much.

Toward morning the flames began to subside and it was a dreadful sight that greeted the dawn. Twisted smoking rubble covered the west side of the street, the vault standing like a grim specter jutting out of the wreckage of the bank building. Sofie and I had been across the street at the hotel making coffee and sandwiches ever since it was certain the fire had been contained. One by one the men straggled in, faces streaked with black smoke. Anxiously I watched for Charlie and David and when they came through the door I dropped what I was doing and ran to them. We clung together, a ragged, heartbroken trio, not minding that everyone was looking on. "There, there dearest, it's only buildings, no lives lost, thanks be to God. It can all be rebuilt," he whispered through cracked and blackened lips. The brilliant blue eyes were red rimmed and dimmed with pain, but they looked into mine with love and I knew then that no matter what life handed us, we would face it with faith in God and each other.

**1998**
The little town by the edge of the slough still stands, and nearing its hundredth year, is remembering the early days. Ravaged by fires, flood, depression and drought, it goes on. Smaller by far, but not beaten yet. Unlike Travare and the many other ghost towns that dot the old maps of Roberts County, Peever, with the determination of its citizens, will move into the new century with hope.

T. H. Peever who founded the town in 1901.

This building is the former Travare Postoffice. Moved to SW of Peever.
The Jarman family lived in this house in the 1960's
when it stood in Easter township.

East side of Main Street Peever.
About 1910. M. OPITZ building still in use. Built in 1902—
author and her husband run a cafe and grocery in it.

Roberts County Courthouse—
after being moved from Travare to Wilmot, 1886.